LOOKING UP

ALSO BY STEPHAN PASTIS

The Trubble Town series

Squirrel Do Bad

The Why-Why's Gone Bye-Bye

Looking Up

STEPHAN PASTIS

Aladdin

New York   London   Toronto   Sydney   New Delhi

ALADDIN

An imprint of Simon & Schuster Children's Publishing Division

1230 Avenue of the Americas, New York, New York 10020

First Aladdin hardcover edition October 2023

Copyright © 2023 by Stephan Pastis

All rights reserved, including the right of reproduction in whole or in part in any form.

ALADDIN and related logo are registered trademarks of Simon & Schuster, Inc.

For information about special discounts for bulk purchases, please contact Simon & Schuster Special Sales at 1-866-506-1949 or business@simonandschuster.com.

The Simon & Schuster Speakers Bureau can bring authors to your live event. For more information or to book an event contact the Simon & Schuster Speakers Bureau at 1-866-248-3049 or visit our website at www.simonspeakers.com.

Cover designed by Karin Paprocki

Interior designed by Mike Rosamilia

The illustrations for this book were rendered digitally.

The text of this book was set in Excelsior LT Std.

Manufactured in the United States of America 0923 BVG

10 9 8 7 6 5 4 3 2 1

Library of Congress Cataloging-in-Publication Data

Names: Pastis, Stephan, author, illustrator.

Title: Looking up / Stephan Pastis.

Description: First Aladdin hardcover edition. | New York : Aladdin, 2023. | Audience: Ages 8 to 12. | Summary: Upset that her neighborhood is being torn down and replaced by fancy condos and coffee shops, Saint, along with her new friend Daniel, hatches a plan to save what is left of her beloved hometown.

Identifiers: LCCN 2023001675 (print) | LCCN 2023001676 (ebook) | ISBN 9781665929622 (hc) | ISBN 9781665929639 (ebook)

Subjects: CYAC: Loneliness—Fiction. | Friendship—Fiction. | City and town life—Fiction. | Single-parent families—Fiction. | Humorous stories. | LCGFT: Humorous fiction. | Novels.

Classification: LCC PZ7.P269422 Lo 2023 (print) | LCC PZ7.P269422 (ebook) | DDC [Fic]—dc23

LC record available at https://lccn.loc.gov/2023001675

LC ebook record available at https://lccn.loc.gov/2023001676

chapter 1

PIN THE TAIL ON THE DANIEL

You know you're a square peg in a round world when you find you're the only person at the birthday party *defending* the piñata.

As I had the tailless donkey.

And the gnome-themed cake.

For I was a sucker for anything with a face.

Its salvation my destiny.

And no face required saving more than the round one belonging to Daniel "Chance" McGibbons.

ROUND FACE

Who had to keep being reminded by his father to stop drawing and at least talk to the other kids at the birthday party.

As it was *his* birthday party.

But the act of talking seemed to pain him almost as much as the pummeling of the piñata pained me.

Though I didn't know why.

For as much as I admired the shape of his adorably round face, I knew next to nothing about him.

Other than the fact that he lived across the street from me. Which was the only reason I had even been *invited* to this gathering of what were otherwise just his classmates.

Who, truth be told, appeared to know as little about Daniel as I did.

Aside from the obvious.

Like the fact that he was the only kid any of us knew who walked with a cane.

Which I thought only old people used.

And which may have been the cause of his shyness.

But whether it was the cane or just an aversion to social events, Daniel's absence as host and birthday boy left a void that could be felt by all, most notably his father. Who seemed as graceful and sociable as Daniel was not. And who wanted Daniel to participate in his birthday party not so much for the sake of Daniel, but for his own desire to not be embarrassed around the other parents.

And sensing Daniel's distress, I stepped in to fill the void. For having ostracized myself among this group of strangers by attempting to save the piñata, donkey, and gnome, I had little left to lose.

And so I climbed atop a barstool in the living room and waxed eloquent.

On the benefits of shopping local.

The merits of print journalism.

And the pitfalls of birthday hats upon soft, malleable hair.

None of which seemed to connect with my peers.

And so I tried to be slightly more topical by saying a few kind words about the birthday boy, who I could see standing behind the other kids, as he had been made to do by his father.

But because I knew so little about him, I could only talk about what I had seen. So I praised his resilience (the cane), his creativity (the drawing), and his listening skills (his silence).

And did not notice until it was too late that each time I said his name, he was taking one giant step backward. As though each word of praise were somehow a lance to the belly.

Until he was left standing with his back against the wall.

Pinned there by unintentional cruelty.

Like the donkey without a tail.

And seeing that I had unwittingly hurt the one round face I'd sought to save, I did the only noble thing I could.

I grabbed the piñata and fled.

chapter 2

EGGSCUSES, EGGSCUSES

The first thing you gotta know about me is that even though my name is Saint, I wasn't named for a bearded guy in heaven.

I was named for a football team in Louisiana.

And the second thing you gotta know about me is this: My mother breaks all her promises.

"Saint, I have a work lunch."

"On a Saturday?"

"Yep."

"So tell them you're sick."

"I can't."

"Tell them your daughter's sick."

"Saint, please."

"Tell them you broke her heart and now she's sneezing uncontrollably."

"Sweetheart—"

"I've got it—tell them your daughter is allergic to broken promises."

My mother knelt on one knee in front of me.

"You know I didn't promise you, Saint. I said I'd go if I could."

"Sounds like a promise to me."

"Please don't make me feel worse than I already do."

"*You?* How about how *I* feel? It's a parent/child egg toss. I can't do it without you."

"Honey, the flyer says it's 'The First Annual Egg Toss.' Which means they'll do it every year. So we'll do it next year."

"But next year is a million years away!" I shouted. "The sky could fall and crush us all by then."

"I doubt that."

"Yeah, well, don't be so sure. Those stars appear to have very little support."

"Hang on," she said, walking to the hall closet and bringing back an umbrella.

"What's that for?" I asked as she opened the umbrella and handed it to me.

"Take it for when you leave the house."

"It's not raining."

"Not for the rain. The stars. They'll hit it and just bounce off."

Now maybe that sounds funny to you. But to me it was just about the most aggravating thing I had ever heard.

Which you wouldn't have known by all my giggling.

"I heard that," said my mother.

And that's the thing about my mother. Whenever you get really angry about something, she goes and makes you laugh. Even if you don't want to.

"I'm still angry," I said.

"You're giggling."

"It's an angry giggle."

"Well, while you angry giggle, I have to go meet a client," she said, grabbing her car keys.

And so I made one last attempt to change her mind.

"You know it's for, like, a hundred thousand dollars, right?"

She stopped and turned around. "What's for a hundred thousand dollars?"

"The egg toss."

"Sweetie, I don't think the winner gets a hundred thousand dollars."

"Well, maybe not a hundred thousand, but they get a shopping spree at Punch's Toy Farm. And that's pretty much worth a hundred thousand dollars. All the toys you can grab in five minutes. I even know the order I'd grab everything. I have the entire layout of the store memorized."

She walked back toward me.

"I'll tell you what. How about I buy you something from Punch's next week? But it's gonna have to be something small. I have just enough cash to buy gas for the car."

She kissed me on the top of my head. Which was always her way of telling me a conversation was over.

"You promise?" I asked.

"Promise," she said.

"Hang on."

"Saint, I have to go."

I ran to my room and came back with a piñata. Not the one I had taken from Daniel's birthday party. But one I had taken from a different party. As I had a habit of saving piñatas.

"Swear on the piñata's head," I said, setting it in front of her.

It was a ritual we performed whenever a promise was sacred and unbreakable. For no one could lie before a creature as fragile as a piñata.

"Saint—"

"Please."

"Fine."

And so she touched the top of the piñata's head.

"I swear on the piñata's head," she said. "And while we're promising things, how about you promise you'll get your chores done? The dishes aren't going to wash themselves."

"Fine," I said. "But first I want to go to the park and watch the egg toss anyway. See what undeserving soul gets the hundred thousand dollars."

"No. First you're doing the dishes."

"Fine."

"And—"

"And what?"

"If you do go, Saint, try to be a good sport. I know what you're like when you're disappointed."

"I promise."

But I hadn't touched the piñata's head.

And she didn't know what Punch's meant to me.

. chapter 3 .

KNIGHTLY PRAYERS

Punch's Toy Farm sat like an old, tired mule on the corner of my street and Miguel Avenue, exactly 1,605 steps away from my front door. (I've counted.)

And don't ask me why it was called Punch's Toy Farm.

Because the owner was not named Punch, and it was in no way a farm.

But those branding difficulties were the least of its problems.

For the old building was plagued by a whole host of issues, including, but not limited to, a leaky roof, broken air-conditioning, and wooden floors so warped you could drop a marble in the Barbie aisle and watch it roll all the way to the front door.

Which only made me love it more.

For those deficiencies were a testament to how long Punch's had endured. A reminder that the store came not from the present but the past.

And the past was the place I liked best.

A feeling shared by the store's only employee.

Whose name was Muffins.

MUFFINS

Muffins was an eighty-six-year-old curmudgeon who loathed children, smelled like cigarettes, and had fingers far too long for his hand.

And despite being the store's only employee, Muffins spent very little time in the store itself. Which meant that if you were a new customer and needed help, you weren't going to find it.

But if you were a veteran shopper, you knew to walk to the back of the store, step over the dusty stacks of shipping receipts, and push open the emergency exit that told you not to do that very thing.

EMERGENCY
EXIT ONLY
ALARM WILL
SOUND

For the alarm had long since been disabled by Muffins, who you would then find behind the store in a rusty lawn chair, spitting sunflower seed shells into a tin bucket.

PING!

But finding Muffins was only half the battle. For you then had to know the rules of engagement.

Like avoiding small talk.

Instead, you were just to say what kind of toy you were looking for. And be brief.

Especially when he asked the only question he ever asked:

"Homework finito?"

Which was his way of inquiring if your homework was done. Because if it wasn't, your shopping *was*.

But if you said yes—and I always said yes—you had to sign a form, which he appeared to have tailored specifically for me.

FORM OF TRUTH

MY HOMEWORK HAS BEEN COMPLETED.
I SWEAR THIS ON THE HEADS OF MY
SACRED PIÑATAS.
Saint

Now I don't remember even telling him about my piñatas, especially given that you weren't supposed to be chatting with him in the first place. Though maybe I had. Or maybe he just had the power to read people's minds.

Anyhow, the point is that when all those formalities were concluded, the ballerina-like grace of Muffins kicked in.

For he would spit his last shell into the bucket, and as the *ping* of the bucket rang, Muffins would slip silently back into the store, where he'd slither through tight aisles, stand upon a squeaky footstool, and reach with his long bony fingers into shelves crammed three rows deep with toys.

To find not just the toy you wanted but the one you *needed*.

And for me, that expertise was a must.

Because of what I collected.

And that was knights.

I had always been drawn to knights for their honor and decency, and for the way they protected the many damsels in distress.

Sort of like how I protected piñatas.

I was also drawn to their boldness and the fact that they were rarely troubled by the what-ifs of a perilous situation. Because if they *did* ever fail—which was rare—they could always just cover their face.

But I didn't collect just *any* knight figurines.

For I had no interest in the cliché ones swinging swords and clanging shields, all of which could be easily bought from any cookie-cutter chain store.

Meh.

Instead, I collected just one particular pose.

And that was the knight bent upon one knee.

THIS ONE.

Now I don't know what the toy makers had in mind with that specific pose, i.e., whether the guy was proposing to a maiden or had simply dropped his house keys.

But I knew what *I* had in mind.

And that was that those knights were asking the gods for help with slaying the dragons—not by violent means, which is also cliché—but by nonviolent means.

And so on my shelf at home, you would often find a praying knight surrounded by dragons who had died of old age and poor hygiene.

FATAL HALITOSIS

Now given my love for anything with a face, you might think it's hypocritical of me to feel that way about dragons.

But consider this:

Those reptiles were going around breathing fire onto knights.

Which to me is crossing an ethical line.

And besides, if you want to get really technical, knights have faces too.

So that's where the ethics of this get murky.

Anyhow, the point is that I couldn't collect *any* of those praying knights without the genius of Muffins. Whose skill at his chosen profession was so profound as to be almost supernatural. An encyclopedic knowledge of toys paired with an ability to see into customers' souls.

And after he'd help me find just the right knight, he would take the toy to the register, next to which there was a rack of picture books, many with castles and knights. And so while he was ringing me up, I'd always throw in one of those, just to expand my knowledge base.

Then I'd gather up all the coins I had gotten from selling lemonade outside my house and pay. And cash was the *only* way to pay.

For the store had tried to install a credit card reader, but Muffins had made sure it did not survive its first day.

Then Muffins would hand me my change and say the only other thing he ever said:

"Don't slam the darn door, dingo."

And then I would leave.

And Muffins would return to his chair.

And all of that is a long way of saying that I really wanted to win that egg toss.

But couldn't because of my mother.

And so I went to the event anyway, and responded to the disappointment in the most mature way I could think of.

By chucking eggs at a tree.

chapter 4

TOSS SOME YELLOW YOLK ON THE OLE OAK TREE

I know what you're gonna say.

Which is that I promised my mother that if I went to the egg toss, I would be a good sport.

But technically that's not correct. Because:

(1) I hadn't sworn on the piñata's head, and

(2) Seeing those happy kids with their parents was more than any reasonable person could take.

Because for one thing, Punch's was *my* store, not theirs.

And for another, their only qualification to even *be* in this contest was that they had a parent who didn't work Saturdays.

And besides, even if one of them did win a shopping spree at Punch's, they wouldn't know a single thing about navigating those uneven floorboards, not to mention making sense of the store's unconventional layout. Because in Punch's, the dolls weren't next to the ponies. They were next to the tanks.

Why? Because that's the way Muffins wanted it.

And don't even get me started on what Muffins's reaction would be to some kid scrambling like a maniac through his aisles. I half expect he would grab them by their orthodontic headgear and hurl them ungently into the good night.

And I did not go gently into that good night either.

Mostly because the whole thing was just so unfair. I mean, what had all those kids done to deserve an egg-tossing parent? Nothing that I could see.

And I knew for a fact they didn't want that prize one millionth as much as I did. Nor did they need it, judging by the fancy new cars they poured out of at the park. And so rather than watch any more happy kids with their parents, I did the next-most-logical thing:

I chucked eggs at a tree.

And I probably would have *kept* throwing eggs at a tree if I hadn't heard a voice come from behind it.

"I wonder if you could do that somewhere else."

And seen a face that I recognized.

"Daniel?" I asked. "What are you doing here?"

"Who are you?" he answered.

"Saint. I live across the street from you."

"You do?"

"Yes," I replied. "I came to your birthday party."

Which I could tell from his blank stare was not registering.

And so I introduced myself by saying the one thing I didn't want to say.

"I'm the girl who stole your piñata."

"Ohhh," he said. "I know you."

And really, I didn't know what to do next. Because

on the one hand, I was upset he hadn't remembered me. And on the other hand, I was embarrassed about the thing he *did* remember. So I didn't know whether to drop the entire subject or apologize for everything. And so I took the middle course:

I became unintelligible.

"I didn't mean to steal it. More like save it. Protect it. Like in a closet. Like the knights. And the damsels. I mean, they didn't have closets. Nor cardboard. Just castles. And moats. Do you like knights? I like knights. And the past. And piñatas. And anything with a face. Like the gnome. And the donkey. Except dragons. All that fire. Faces. Closet. Tree."

And at that point, I didn't even know what was happening.

I was just spewing out random nouns like a typewriter gone rogue.

Because something about Daniel's round face made me dizzier than eating a bowl of Peppy Pops.

Fortunately, Daniel cut me off with a question that was direct but thoughtful.

ME ON PEPPY POPS

PEPPY POPS

"Why are you throwing eggs at a tree?"

And I even blew that.

"Because my mother breaks her promises."

"Huh?"

And forcing myself to get it together before I frightened him into fleeing, I took a deep breath and uttered something that could fairly be called a sentence.

"My mother was supposed to take me. You know, so we could compete in the egg toss. But she had to work. So I'm here by myself."

"Oh."

"Are you here with your dad?" I asked.

"My dad?"

"Yeah. I met him at your birthday party."

"Oh. That wasn't my dad. That was my uncle."

"Your uncle?"

"I live with him."

And I don't know what it was about hearing him say that, but suddenly I felt a kinship with him. A bond. Like it was me and him against the universe.

Except only one of us knew it.

"Do you mind if I draw?" he asked.

"Not at all!" I said, much too excitedly, given what he said next.

"By myself."

"Oh. Yeah. Sure. I'm sorry."

"It's just hard to concentrate when I have to talk."

"Of course."

"And I usually don't talk this much."

"Right, right," I answered. "I don't like talking much either."

Which made no sense given that just two minutes prior I had spouted off a majority of the nouns in the English language.

And that's where I should have just said goodbye.
But I didn't.

Instead, I said this:

"I have a turtle."

"Huh?"

"A painted turtle."

"Oh."

"He eats lettuce."

"Okay," he said. "But I'm gonna draw now."

"Oh yeah, don't mind me. Sorry. That's the last thing I wanted to say. It's just, like, the only reason I'm even saying it is that you live right across the street, and if you ever want to feed him, I can probably arrange that. I mean, he's not big on strangers, but if emotionally he feels a kinship, he would probably be amenable. You know, like, he'd be open to you, and the feeding, and maybe even a deeper relationship. If, of course, that's what you wanted."

"Right," he answered.

And it was then that I saw his drawing of an oak tree, Spanish moss hanging from its branches like the uncombed hair of an old woman. And I was just about to tell him it was the most beautiful drawing I had ever seen, when suddenly I noticed something else on the drawing.

Egg yolk.

Which must have splattered onto the canvas from one of my many throws, smearing every bit of ink it touched.

"I'm so sorry," I said.

But he didn't answer.

"Maybe I can clean it off."

But I don't even think he heard me. Instead, he

just snatched up all his pens and paper like they were in the path of a charging elephant.

"Don't leave," I pleaded. "I'm really sorry. I didn't mean to do it. Really."

And leaning his body weight upon his cane to stand upright, he said only one thing:

"Please just leave me alone."

chapter 5

UNPROMISED LAND

The only reason I didn't cry all the way home was that my mother picked me up from the park, and I didn't want to have to explain all the dumb things I had done.

Plus, she had a surprise.

"The reason I picked you up is to take you to Mrs. Trifaldi's house."

"Old Lady Trifaldi's house? What for?"

"She's having a party."

"*She's* having a party?"

"Yeah. Why, does that seem odd to you?"

And it did.

Because for one thing, Old Lady Trifaldi lived in one of the oldest homes in our neighborhood.

MRS. TRIFALDI'S HOUSE

And for another thing, she was dead.

TRIFALDI
R.I.P.

Or at least *used to be* dead.

And then somehow un-died.

That is, if you believed all the rumors about the strange lady in the old house. Of which there were many.

There was even some talk she was now just a ghost—a belief fueled by the fact that she could sometimes be seen late at night on her roof.

Which seemed like something a ghost would do.

All of which made the notion of her having a party at least a tad bit unexpected.

"So what's the party for?" I asked my mother.

"It's an after-party for all the contestants."

"The egg-toss contestants?"

"Yep."

"But I wasn't a contestant," I said.

"Well, it's not *just* for the contestants. It's for everyone. I think she wants to do something nice for the neighborhood."

"Are you going with me?"

"I can't. I just left the meeting I was at to pick you up. But I gotta get back to it."

"So the party's *not* really for everyone."

"Let's not do this again, Saint. You're gonna have a great time."

But I was still upset over my mother not participating in the egg toss, not to mention what had happened with Daniel. And so I said:

"I'm not going."

"Saint, you told me yourself you always wanted to see the inside of her house. You like old houses. And besides, she's selling it. So if you don't see it now, you probably never will."

"Why? Who's gonna live in it after?"

"Nobody. It'll be torn down for something new."

"What? Why?"

"It's in bad shape, and I don't think anyone wants to spend the money to fix it."

"What a waste," I answered. "Old stuff is always better."

But my mother wasn't listening.

Because just as I said it, her old car coughed twice and died. And whenever that happened, she had to pull it over and give it a few moments of rest.

Like it was an old, tired pony.

OLD, TIRED PONY

"Old," she said as the car rested, "is not always better." And, taking a deep breath, she took her hands off the steering wheel. "Well, while we wait here, I have something I should probably tell you. And don't get all freaked out on me."

Which ensured that whatever she said next would cause me to freak out on her.

"I can't take you shopping at Punch's next week. It has to be the week after."

"You're breaking your promise."

"No, Saint. I'm moving it forward a week."

"And then you'll move it forward another week. You always do that."

"I won't."

"You don't know that," I said. "No one knows what's gonna happen in the future. It's even worse than the present."

"I promised to take you shopping at Punch's and I will."

"You swore on the piñata!"

"Saint, I have a broken-down car and a meeting I'm gonna be late for. This is not a good time."

"It's never a good time with you," I said.

And you know sometimes when you talk to your mom and it's a regular old argument, but then you say that one thing or raise your voice—and boom, the whole thing goes south?

Well, this was that thing.

"Keep talking to me like that and you watch what happens," she said, with a hissing tone that could make cats flee up trees.

CAT UP TREE

"Oh yeah?" I answered.

"Yeah. How about I don't take you at all?"

"Fine," I said, opening the passenger door. "I don't want you to take me anyway."

"Where are you going?"

"I'm walking to the party," I answered, slamming the car door. "It's two blocks away."

She took a deep breath.

"Get back in the car, Saint. I'm driving you there."

"No, I want to be by myself."

"What for?"

"So you won't get a chance to break any more promises."

chapter 6

CRASHING THE PARTY

With all that had happened with the egg toss and Daniel and my mother, I was determined to have an epically bad time at Old Lady Trifaldi's party.

That is, if she hadn't answered the door dressed as cheese.

"Great," she said. "You're here."

"You know me?" I asked.

"No. But I know you're just about the right size to wear this."

"What is it?"

"A mask—what does it look like?"

"So this is a costume party?" I asked.

"No."

"Then why are we dressing up?"

"I'm dressing up because it's laundry day. And this is the only clean thing I had."

"So why do *I* have to dress up?"

"You don't *have* to. It's a privilege. I'm making you the Winged Skull o' Doom, head of the Skeleton Krewe. Decrier of merriment."

"What's that?"

"Too many questions," she answered, handing me the mask. "Just try this on."

Which I did.

"Perfect," she said. "It fits. Now go forth and hurl curses upon the heads of all those merrymakers inside."

"Huh?" I replied. "What for?"

"Because the Skeleton Krewe is jealous of the living! Angry over their time-wasting parties."

"But aren't you the one holding the party?"

"Yes."

"So then why are you—?"

"Because I'm a lonely old lady! Now go forth and curse!"

"But what do I say?"

"How do I know?" she answered.

"It was your idea."

"Say something *bad*."

"Like, 'May the stars fall down upon your miserable heads'?"

"No, no, no, no," she said. "Nothing *that* bad. Although they'd deserve it."

"Because they're miserable people?"

"They are?" she asked.

"Well, you said they deserve it."

"Yes, but I don't know if they're miserable. I just know they're new to the neighborhood. And I don't like new people. I'm old. I don't like change."

"So what do I say to them?"

"I don't know—curse them with stubbed toes. Lost keys. Bad haircuts."

I turned to go, but stopped.

"I don't like change either," I confided. "And I'm not even old."

She paused and looked at me thoughtfully. *"JUST GO FORTH AND CURSE!"*

And so I began wandering through the party, where I fit in about as well as a hearse at a Christmas parade.

And without the heart to hurl curses upon people I barely knew, I chose instead to explore Old Lady Trifaldi's home, stopping in her parlor, mostly because it had no people, but also because it had a large portrait of her.

Which only became unusual when one looked at the bottom, where one could see a skeleton's hand rising from the ground and grabbing her around the ankle.

And after staring at the painting for a good ten minutes, I couldn't decide if Old Lady Trifaldi *had* died or *hadn't*.

Or had died but had come back as cheese.

For the reality of Old Lady Trifaldi was far stranger than the rumors.

About the only thing I *did* know was that it was hot inside my skull mask. And so I took it off and sat in a chair beside the fireplace. Where I noticed a glossy brochure.

It seemed to be all about the town's plans for a new this and a new that. So I put it into my pocket to read later, hoping it could shed some light on why anyone would tear down a house as old as this.

"Well, do I have a bone to pick with you!" barked a voice from behind me.

So I turned around to see one of the children's fathers holding an armful of toys.

"Get it?" he asked. "I just love puns. I can keep going if you want."

"It's okay," I said.

"Great costume, by the way. Mind if I use that table over there?" he asked. "Just looking for a place I can put all these toys. I'm Trevor's dad."

But I didn't know any Trevors.

"We won the egg toss. He just finished his little shopping spree."

"It's over already?" I asked.

"Yup."

I looked through his poor selection of toys, which consisted mostly of generic trains a person could have bought anywhere. And I mean *anywhere*.

"Someone should have talked to me," I said, shaking my head. "These aren't even valuable."

"Uh-oh," he said. "Did he make a *grave* error?" He paused. "Okay. I'll stop."

"It's no joke," I said. "I know every inch of that store. I know it better than my own closet. I could have told him right where to go. For the *really* valuable stuff. Not this cookie-cutter clutter. He should have at least consulted with me."

"Well, he likes trains. So I think he's pretty happy with what he got. Besides, everyone was in a bit of a hurry. They had to clear the store out after."

"What do you mean, 'clear it out'?"

"Empty the shelves. Get ready for the big show."

"They had a show?"

"Well, not a *show* show. Just a big boom."

"I don't know what you're talking about."

"Punch's."

"What about it?"

"You don't know?"

"KNOW WHAT?" I said.

"They demolished it this afternoon to make room for a coffee shop."

Suddenly, I felt so dizzy I thought I would collapse.

"Amazing how fast those crews can work," he added.

And without thinking, I put the skull mask back on.

And said the only thing I could.

"May the stars fall down upon your miserable head."

chapter 7

RUBBLE, RUBBLE, YOUR TOWN IS A MESS

I was so shocked and disoriented by the news about Punch's that I walked all the way home and forgot to take off my mask.

And it wasn't just the loss of the toy store that was shocking.

It was the loss of Muffins.

MUFFINS

Who I somehow knew I would never see again.

Which leads me to a question I would someday like an answer to:

Where do people you've known go after they're gone?

My guess is they all gather in the same spot somewhere and probably have a party. But you never get invited. So that makes it hurt all the more. And that makes me think you should never get too close to anyone, because they'll just leave and go to that party you can't attend.

But that's neither here nor there.

The point is that after leaving Old Lady Trifaldi's, I didn't know what to do.

Part of me was hoping that Trevor's father was wrong and that I just needed to go to Punch's and find out for myself.

But I couldn't.

Because I knew that if I walked past it and saw a heap of rubble, I would fall right down like that building and cry for the rest of my life.

Plus, I knew he wasn't wrong.

Because the same thing that had apparently happened to Punch's was happening throughout our town. And had happened to every old home on my block, which one by one went up for sale and one by one disappeared.

Except for ours.

Which now stood like a structural orphan in a sea of weeds.

It was like the entire town I loved and the people I loved were disappearing right before my eyes. Replaced by new things and new people, none of which I liked half as much as the old.

Which raised another question:

Why is everyone so eager to replace the past with the present? Because if you want to know the truth, I'd rather make time move backward than forward, and leave the whole present out of it.

For the present left me too sad to cry.

And unsure of what to do next.

Because normally when I was this down, I would go to the shelf in my bedroom where I kept the knights and see to it that a few more dragons expired.

FAILED TO FLOSS DAILY

But this was much worse.

And so I did the only thing I could do when faced with a situation so dire.

I held a pity party in my closet with my piñatas.

And though their hearts were filled with candy and mine with sadness, together we were a band of brothers.

Who, as the town tightened its grip around us, tightened our grip around each other.

Because in the end, it was all about what I had said to my mother—that in the short time between promises and the future, the sky can fall.

Which had now happened.

To the one place I loved more than anywhere else on earth.

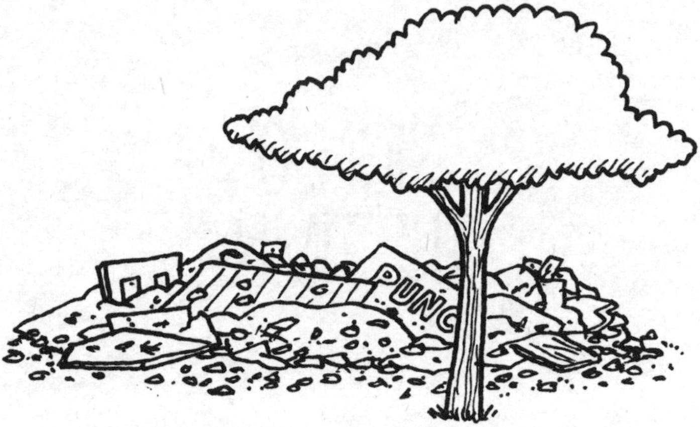
PUNC

And so I sat in my closet with my piñatas, resigned to both my town's fate and my own. Ready for the wrecking ball that had tolled for Punch's to soon toll for us.

When suddenly I was saved by Dr. Rutherford B. Hayes.

. chapter 8 .

SIGN O'
THE TIMES

It's hard to believe I've told you this much about me while barely even mentioning my life partner, Dr. Rutherford B. Hayes.

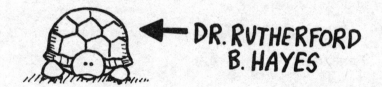

DR. RUTHERFORD B. HAYES

Dr. Rutherford B. Hayes is a painted turtle that I found in a dry creek bed.

I originally named him "Rocks," due to the fact that he is so antisocial he rarely emerges from his shell, thereby making him look more like a rock than a reptile.

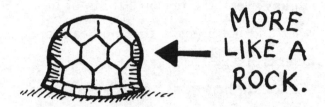

MORE LIKE A ROCK.

But he was insulted by the name, which he called "jejune," a word I do not know that you will just have to look up for yourself.

And don't ask me why he wanted to be called "Dr. Rutherford B. Hayes" either.

Because all I know is that Rutherford B. Hayes was the nineteenth president of the United States, had a very long beard, and was—to the best of my knowledge—not a doctor.

RUTHERFORD B. HAYES →

VERY LONG BEARD (NOT A DOCTOR)

In any event, the reason I think of him as a life partner and not a pet is that he bears none of the hallmarks of a pet.

For Dr. Rutherford B. Hayes will not:

- Fetch,
- Snuggle,
- Guard the house,
- Do tricks, or
- Jog beside you on a leash.

All of which might cause you to ask why I wanted him to be my life partner in the first place.

And that was because of his wisdom.

For Dr. Rutherford B. Hayes knows 381,434 of the 470,874 entries in *Webster's Third New International Dictionary*.

Which I know because I asked.

And he was only too happy to answer.

For if Dr. Rutherford B. Hayes has any fault at all, it is that he can sometimes be arrogant.

Which I pointed out only once, after which he called me a name I did not understand but presumed to be horrific.

And so I made it a rule to never point out his shortcomings, and instead accept him for the brilliant counselor that he is.

And thus when he would climb upon the rock at the top of his aquarium (known as Plato's Profound Perch—his term, not mine), I would listen.

PLATO'S PROFOUND PERCH

And when I told him about Punch's and explained that I didn't know where to turn next, he gave me his advice.

And that advice was one word:

Chance.

As in Daniel "Chance" McGibbons.

But just like with the big words he used, I did not understand.

And so he explained that the same thing that had happened on our side of the street had happened on *Daniel's* side of the street as well—each of the houses around him had been bought and torn down—leaving his house as the lone one still standing.

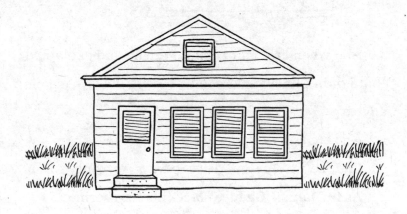

And thus my turtle realized in all his wisdom that Daniel and I were fated to be natural allies.

For in a battle like this, two were better than one.

And while I couldn't save Punch's, I could take all the anger I now had inside me and do something with it by working with Daniel to at least save that which was still left.

Like his house and mine.

Which to me seemed like just about the smartest idea anyone had ever had.

Except for one small detail:

DANIEL LOATHED ME LIKE A DISEASE.

For despite my good intentions, my only inter- actions with him had involved the splattering of his artwork with egg yolk and the theft of his birthday piñata.

And so I sat by my bedroom window staring out toward his house for hours on end, hopeless as could be, but secretly wishing that he would somehow see the wisdom of our super-duo pairing on his own.

Which of course didn't happen.

And I know what you're saying—*maybe that was because Daniel was fine with the whole town changing. Maybe he didn't care about the homes on our block. Maybe he didn't care about Punch's.*

To which I say:

And also:

Because the truth was I didn't know *how* Daniel
felt. For I had been too busy throwing eggs at him to
inquire.

I could only hope that one day there would be some change in his circumstance that might affect him the way the loss of Punch's had me.

And then one day there was.

In the form of a sign.

Not from the gods, but a real estate office.

Stuck right there in his yard.

chapter 9

KNIGHT SWEATS

Isn't it odd how sometimes you feel really bad, and then you wake up the next morning and it's like you're a whole different person?

Well, that was me the next day.

In fact, I was so happy, I even resuscitated a few dragons.

For I knew I finally had my opportunity to approach Daniel.

But as much as I wanted to sprint across the street immediately, I knew I had to be smart about it.

Because given what I had done to him so far, there was no reason for him to talk to me, much less trust me.

And that's when it hit me.

The way to change all that.

To convince him that I was a person he could not only trust but admire.

And using an abundance of cardboard I had purchased from Tippy's Piñata Paradise to save it from becoming piñatas, as well as some flair from Old Lady Trifaldi, I fashioned the appropriate outfit.

And boldly knocked at Daniel's door.

But no one answered.

Which maybe is why knights rarely knocked, but instead bashed down doors.

And waiting there on the porch under the hot sun, I became aware that the biggest threat to a knight was not a sword to the heart, but the heat inside cardboard.

And so I took off my helmet, which had not been kind to my soft, malleable hair.

And that's when the door opened.

And I looked like this:

Now in all my books about knights, this was the moment when the damsel in distress usually fainted with joy and the knight caught her and carried her far away from the giants or the dragons or whatever horrible thing was after her. After which she'd awake and wrap her long arms around his neck and say, "Ye are my hero."

But instead, Daniel said:

OH GOD, IT'S YOU.

And I replied by saying something very awkward, which in retrospect probably did not have to be uttered in Medieval English.

THOUEST PERMIT MY ENTRY ACROSS YE DRAWBRIDGE?

"Why are you here?" he asked.

"To save us both."

"From what?"

"Ye are my Daniel in Distress!"

"I don't get it."

"It doesn't matter," I said. "The point is that I'm a knight."

"Okay."

"That means you can trust me."

"To do what?"

"The right thing."

And then he paused, no doubt contemplating just what to say in a moment as grand as this.

Which turned out to be:

"No offense, but I'm gonna go back inside now."

Now I don't know about you, but whenever somebody says "no offense," the next thing they say is always offensive.

And leaving me to die of sunstroke was at least a tad bit offensive.

"Wait," I said, before he could shut the door. "I'm really hot. Can I at least have a glass of water?"

And though he didn't say I could come inside,

neither did he say no. Instead, he just sighed and walked back into the house, leaving the front door open, which I took as an invitation to cross the non-existent drawbridge.

After which Daniel led me through empty rooms to the kitchen, where he took the lone glass left in the cupboard, filled it with tap water, and offered it to me.

Which if you ask me was pretty darn kind for a Daniel in Distress.

Though I couldn't help noticing the glass, on which was the chipped image of a cat and the cheesy sentence "*CAT* stop loving you."

It was the kind of corny, back-of-the-cupboard glass you only use when all the others are in the dishwasher.

Or when—

"We're moving," he said. "Everything's all packed up. Including the cups."

And there was something so vulnerable about him saying it that I wanted to hug his beautifully round face right there.

But nowhere in my knight books did anyone hug anyone. Probably due to all that armor.

And I had already made such a bad impression with my cube-shaped hair and medieval dialect that I didn't want to worsen things.

"So what are you supposed to be saving me from?" he asked.

Which was just the opening I had been waiting for.

And so I handed him the speech Dr. Rutherford B. Hayes had dictated to me.

It was specifically designed to stir men's souls, but it used too many big words.

And so I had to translate it in the margins:

FROM THE BRILLIANT MIND OF
RUTHERFORD B. HAYES

DR.

    SOMETIMES THE PLAINTIVE CRY OF LIFE IS UNBEARABLE, SEIZING YOU IN ITS VISE-LIKE TENTACLES WITH A MERCILESS FERVOR BORN OF MENACE.

↖ Life bad.

    IT IS IN THOSE SOLITARY DAYS THAT ONE MUST FIND SOLACE IN THE KNOWLEDGE THAT ALL THE EDIFICES OF OUR DREAMS WERE CONSTRUCTED NOT BY THE PUSILLANIMOUS, BUT BY FOREBEARERS WHO SHOWED NO FORBEARANCE.

↖ No idea.

    INDEED, THOSE FOREBEARERS STROVE FOR AN INCANDESCENT GLORY THAT WAS ALMOST TRANSCENDENT — MINDFUL THAT YOU, THEIR HEIR, WOULD ONE DAY BE ITS BENEFICIARY. ↖ Someone did something.

"None of this makes any sense," he said. "Also, why are you dressed like a knight?"

And I wanted to tell him all about what was happening in the neighborhood, and with Punch's Toy Farm, and Mrs. Trifaldi's house, and now his house, and how I was dressed as a knight because knights saved people from harm, and I wanted to save *him* from harm, not to mention *me* from harm, and I wanted to apologize for the piñata and the egg yolk and just about everything else, but each of those thoughts raced for my mouth all at once and my words got bottled up like cars on a rush-hour freeway.

And what came out of my mouth next was undoubtedly the most awkward, nonsensical, grammatically incorrect thing that anyone has ever said in the history of time.

Which was this:

"Me. Love. Your round face. Thanks."

It was at that point I became so mortified that I grabbed my knight's helmet and put it back on my head, in the faint hope that if I covered my face quickly enough, he might forget who I was.

But he didn't. Instead, he made it one billion times worse.

"Is that why you're always staring at our house?"

And right then I wanted to jump into the non-existent moat that surrounded Daniel's dwelling and either float away or drown. Because that's about the most humiliating thing a person can ever ask you. And it caught me so off guard that before I knew it, I was making a claim so outrageous that even *I* couldn't believe it.

"If you must know, I work part-time with the police department doing neighborhood watch."

Only it was even worse than that. Because I was so flustered, I began the sentence by saying, "If *ye* must know."

But then he didn't say anything at all.

And that made me even more nervous.

So then I blurted out this:

"You'll be happy to know that your house is secure."

And this:

"Does it really seem like I stare at you all the time?"

And this:

"I normally do not sweat like a pig in mittens."

It was a display so inept that I half hoped the police would come and arrest me for the stolen piñata.

But they didn't.

And all I could think was how dumb it was for me to even *hope* I could save Daniel.

For maybe he *liked* the thought of moving.

And maybe he *liked* the cat glass.

And maybe he just wanted the girl who had run off with his piñata to stop injecting her square head into his otherwise okay life.

And so I rose to leave.

And that was the moment he dropped his head into his hands and said:

I DON'T WANT TO LEAVE THIS HOUSE.

And *that* Daniel I could save.

chapter 10

YOU SAY IT'S YOUR BIRTHDAY

Seeing Daniel so sad in that big empty house he didn't want to leave was more than I could take. And so I snapped out of the nervous haze I was in, determined to cheer him up.

By taking him to the classiest place I knew:

The Beefy Bee.

The Beefy Bee was a graffiti-covered hamburger stand in a town that was now mostly kale and poké bowls. A grease-spattered loner.

It was run by a man named Spiro, who we all just called Sparrow. Whose burgers came with lettuce, pickles, and onions. And who, if you asked him to hold any of the three, would say:

For Sparrow loathed special orders and special people. And a special person was anyone who complained.

And no complaints bothered him more than the ones about his exit policy, which was as follows:

When you're done eating, you exit.

Because Sparrow had other customers. And the minute you were done eating, you were no longer one of them. And so when you swallowed that last fry, Sparrow would swoop in, grab your wrappers, and cry, "Bye-bye now!" as he pushed you with his other hand toward the door.

And I didn't want that to happen to me and Daniel.

So I gathered up all the change I had left from my lemonade sales and bought Daniel a drink and the largest order of fries I could afford.

And sitting outside at one of Sparrow's tables, I told Daniel everything I had learned about what was happening to our town, most of which I had gleaned from the real estate brochure I'd found at Old Lady Trifaldi's house.

And that was this:

Our town was being invaded by an army of people who were better dressed than us, better educated than us, and better at sipping lattes than us. In theory, they had jobs, but it was difficult to tell given the amount of time they spent sipping lattes.

And yet somehow they had cash.

Oodles of cash.

Brought here under cover of a starless night in a convoy of money trucks.

And all that loot tempted the poor people of our town like cheese to a mouse.

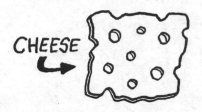

CHEESE

Tempted them to sell their homes.

Tempted them to move their families.

Tempted them to abandon our town.

"But can't they just refuse to sell?" asked Daniel.

"And say no to all that money? No chance," I explained. "Adults love money even more than mice love cheese."

"How sad," said Daniel.

"Yes," I answered, pleased he was finally grasping the depravity of the situation.

And so I explained how, one by one, the places in this town were being bought up and replaced with things that were newer and shinier, with no regard for that which was lost. Like Punch's.

"So what do we do?" asked Daniel.

"We fight back."

"But didn't you say Punch's was already gone?"

"Yes. But you and your house are still here. And I'm gonna make sure you don't disappear on me too."

"But how?"

"The first step is the signs."

"What signs?"

"The ones they put in our yards."

"Like at my house?"

"Right. They can't sell a place if no one knows it's for sale. So I've taken steps to at least slow that down."

"What kind of steps?"

"I can't be specific at this time. But rest assured, it's both legal and professional."

DUMPING THEM IN CREEK.

FOR SALE

FOR SALE
FOR SALE
FOR SALE

It was then that I noticed another crisis unfolding:

For Daniel had finished his french fries.

And if Sparrow noticed it, we would both be booted from The Beefy Bee. Which would interrupt our strategy session at a critical juncture.

"Hang on," I told him. "I need to get you more fries. *Now.*"

"I can get them," he said.

"You're my guest. And a knight of the round table is nothing if not gracious."

And so I went back to the window and ordered more.

"Three dollars," said Sparrow.

And that's when I discovered I had no more money.

Which was a problem.

Until I remembered the one courtesy that Sparrow extended to regular customers.

And so I took advantage.

Because going to The Beefy Bee on your birthday entitled you to one free item from the menu.

Though it wasn't my birthday.

Nor had it been on any of the other six times I had said so.

And if that sounds like an easy way to get free food, it wasn't. Because before you got anything, you had to endure Sparrow's interrogation.

"You lying to Sparrow?" he asked.

"I am not," I answered.

"Sparrow thinks you're lying."

"I'm not."

"Sparrow thinks you are."

"Sparrow is incorrect."

"Look at Sparrow."

Then you would look at Sparrow as he pondered your face, hoping to detect some measure of mendacity in the crinkle of your nose.

And if you didn't crack, he'd give you the food.

Now that might seem bad because it involves lying and all that, but if you want to know the truth, Sparrow knew I was lying.

Which I realized by the time I left and he said, "You age like dog. Seven years in one year."

And so I returned to the table and handed Daniel the fries.

"So what do we do next?" he asked, shoving a handful of fries into his mouth. "Get someone to remove the 'For Sale' sign from my yard?"

"No," I answered. "That just buys us time. This time we need to go bigger."

"Bigger how?"

"This time we stop the sale."

chapter 11.

THE LEERS
OF A CLOWN

Chuck Les Homes was named for its two founders, Chuck and Les.

And it was a name that, if you were driving fast enough down the highway and saw it on a billboard, looked an awful lot like the word "Chuckles."

And that made it sound less like a real estate office and more like a clown school.

An impression that was further reinforced by all the balloons and confetti on their billboard.

And it was their FOR SALE signs that were invading our town.

And so to combat them, we journeyed into the heart of the clown.

Where we sat down at the first desk we found, that of real estate agent James "Baby" Bellachi.

Who looked at me and said, "That looks like it would be very hot to wear on your head."

It was an unprovoked attack.

And set an unnecessarily combative tone for the meeting.

"I am fine," I answered.

"Feel free to take it off if you want."

"I chooseth not."

"Alrighty then," he said, reaching toward a water-cooler behind his desk to fill two small Dixie cups, which he then handed to both of us.

"Water?" he asked.

And I really did want it, sweating as I was. But then I realized I would have to take off my helmet to drink it.

"I regretfully decline," I responded.

"I still want mine," said Daniel.

"And who are you?" he replied, watching Daniel sip from his paper cup.

"He's my associate," I answered for Daniel. "Daniel McGibbons. And we're here because he's decided to not sell his house."

"He owns a house?"

"Yes," I replied. "You see, James 'Baby' Bellachi, my associate here has changed his mind regarding the sale."

"What's the address of the house?" he asked. "I'll look it up."

"1547 Alcala," Daniel answered.

"Let's see now, 1547 Alcala," said the man, glancing at his computer screen. "Ah, yes, charming fixer-upper."

"Thank you," Daniel replied.

"And you live there with your dad, Richard McGibbons?"

"Uncle," he said. "But yes, I live with him."

"And he'd like to keep it that way, James 'Baby' Bellachi."

"You can just call me Jim," he said. "And by the way, what is your name?"

I paused, unprepared for the aggressive inquiry.

"I don't feel comfortable disclosing that at the present time."

"Alrighty then," he said, staring at his computer

screen. "Well, Daniel, it looks like we're out of luck here. The only name on the title is your uncle's. Which means he's the only person with whom we can discuss all that. So if you don't want the house to be sold, your best bet is to talk to him."

Daniel looked at me, helpless.

And seeing those eyes, I wanted nothing more than to strike James "Baby" Bellachi with my lance.

But instead, I said:

"That won't be possible."

"You mean he can't talk to his uncle?"

"I mean we'd like to settle this without his involvement."

"But he's the owner."

"Right," I said, winking.

"Do you have something in your eye?" he asked.

And that's when I put all the birthday money I had been saving right on top of his desk. Four dollars and fifty-five cents.

"How 'bout you pull some strings, James 'Baby' Bellachi?"

He looked at the money and then back at me.

I winked again.

"I'm afraid I don't understand," he said.

"May I?" I asked, grabbing a sheet of paper from his desk and writing on it.

"'Ebirb,'" he said as he read my note. "I don't get it."

"I think it spells 'bribe' backward," interjected Daniel, unaware of the legal ramifications of uttering the word aloud.

"Nope nope nope," I said, tearing the evidence into dozens of pieces and throwing them onto the office carpet.

"Maybe it's time for you two to go," said James "Baby" Bellachi, who, as he rose from his chair, proved to be taller than I'd expected.

And so I made myself taller by standing on his chair.

And, anticipating a joust, I knew the important thing was to strike first and hard.

"James 'Baby' Bellachi, our entire town is being overrun by a race of cookie-cutter foes who favor five-dollar lattes and hot-stone massages and who use their vast store of cheese to lure us from the sanctity of our homes—creaky, leaky homes that we love like an old teddy bear without arms—and from which we emerge each and every day only to find more and more of your 'For Sale' signs set there under cover of a starless night by people with big trucks who value nothing so much as look-alike coffee chains. But our town *is* different, James 'Baby' Bellachi. And yes, maybe Muffins spits seeds and Sparrow needs turnover and Mrs. Trifaldi shouts curses, but the blood that runs through their veins is worth more than that of all those latte-sipping foes put together. For it is ours."

And suddenly infused with a knight's sense of purpose, I grabbed him by his lapels.

"So join us, James 'Baby' Bellachi. Say no to the latte-sippers. Throw your body upon the gears of the machinery and for once in the history of this balloon-festooned clown school *do something that is not in the service of cheese.*"

And there, with my hands still affixed to his lapels, James "Baby" Bellachi looked back at me with the soulful eyes of a convert.

As his mouth mumbled:

"I have no idea what you just said."

And he turned to his secretary and whispered, "Will you please go get Karen?"

And I turned to Daniel and said:

"Run like your life depends on it."

"Why?" he asked.

"'Cause it does."

chapter 12

DRAWING CONCLUSIONS

"My leg is starting to hurt," Daniel said after we had fled halfway across town, him with a cane, and me with a lance.

"Let's duck into there," I said, pointing to the creek bed down the hill. "It's a good place for fugitives."

And so we ran down to the dry creek, where Daniel saw for the first time what I had been doing with the Chuck Les FOR SALE signs.

"Did you do all this?" Daniel asked.

"For legal reasons, I'll have to deny that. But yes, this is clearly where someone is throwing them."

"So why'd we have to run out of the office like that?"

"We had no choice."

"But why?" he asked.

"Because."

"Because why?"

And I don't know whether I was drained from the Battle of Chuck Les or just plain hungry, but either way, I did something a knight should never do—I snapped at my Daniel in Distress.

"You know, I'm sorry, but I'm doing all this to help you. And you just sit there. Like at The Beefy Bee, scarfing down those birthday fries. Or at that real estate office, where you drank from your Dixie cup while I did everything I could to try to save you. You—who in all the time you've lived across the street from me—have never once crossed that street to meet the girl who was staring out her window in the hope that you would pay some attention to her, but never did, until now, when you're scared about your situation. Which, if you ask me, is just a wee bit selfish. So you know what, Daniel McGibbons, maybe you should start answering questions."

And as soon as I'd said it, I wanted to sink into a deep murky bog.

GLUG
GLUG
GLUG

Because the thing about being a knight is that you're supposed to endure everything gracefully, be it arrows, armies, or plague.

And here I got a rumbly in my tumbly and snapped.

And to make matters worse, Daniel didn't snap back.

Instead, he just looked at me with that big round face, and I swear, it was everything I could do to not wrap my arms around his wonderful head.

"I'm sorry," he said quietly.

"You're sorry?" I answered. "I'm the one who has to apologize. I may be the worst knight ever. Feel free to fling me from a catapult back to whatever castle I came from."

And for the first time ever, I heard Daniel giggle.

And it was just about the cutest thing I'd ever heard.

And so that made me giggle too.

"I need to draw that someday," he said. "You flying through the air like that."

"I'd like to see that," I replied. "Just don't make my hair all smooshed from the helmet. Also, you should know that it's very hard to capture my essence."

And with that, Daniel suddenly began to talk.

And so I listened.

"When my uncle took me in, it was kinda weird. Because I didn't really know him. I mean, he was my mom's brother and all, but I don't think they were close. So we never visited him or anything. All I really knew was that he was a travel writer or something. That's why he's gone so much."

And as much as I wanted to ask about what had happened to his father and mother, I could tell he didn't want to talk about it. Ditto his need for a cane. Though I suspected the two things were related.

"And so I'm home by myself a lot. I mean, sometimes I have a babysitter. But I'm mostly alone during the day."

And I wasn't about to interrupt, but part of me was tempted to say how silly it was that he was alone all that time while I was right there across the street and

REALLY WOULD HAVE ENJOYED HIS COMPANY.

But instead, I said nothing.

"I guess it *is* a little strange being alone that much," he continued. "But it's not like my uncle doesn't take care of me. Like, if he's gonna come home late, he leaves me dinner in the fridge. So it's not like I don't have food and stuff. I don't know. I mean, I don't want to complain. He's just busy. And he didn't *have* to take me in. And if he hadn't, who knows what would have happened to me? I probably would have been shipped to some home for bad kids or something."

"I don't think that's a thing," I told him.

"How do you know?"

"Because I'd already be there."

Which seemed to convince him.

"I just really want to draw," he said. "I don't care much about anything else."

"Does he draw with you?"

"My uncle?"

"Yeah."

"No. We don't really *do* much together."

"Why not?"

"I don't know if he would care very much about the things I like."

"Like your drawing and all that?"

"Imaginative stuff. I dunno. I just like thinking up new characters and stories. Plus, when I draw at home, I feel like the world can't get me."

And that's the thing about Daniel. Just when you think he's gonna clam up and not say another word, he goes and says something like that.

"What does that mean?" I asked.

"You know, bad stuff, bad things. I'm safe where I draw. That's why I don't want to move."

"You draw in your bedroom?"

He shook his head. "Different room."

"Can I see it one day?"

"Maybe. I dunno. I don't really show it to anyone else."

"But don't you get lonely in there? You can't meet other people like that."

"Like who?"

"Like me."

Which, right after I said it, I wished I hadn't, because the first time we met I pilfered his piñata.

"Right," he said. "I suppose. But every new person you meet is someone the world can one day take away."

And then I didn't know *what* to say.

Because on the one hand, it was my knightly duty to make him feel better.

But on the other hand, I agreed.

And I wanted to tell him my theory about how all the people who have left you were somehow all together at this big party. The one you can't attend. And how it's really pathetic.

But it didn't feel like the moment for that.

"Sorry I never came out of my house and said hi to you," he mumbled with his head down.

"You don't have to apologize, Daniel."

He looked up at me. "Is it okay if I ask *you* something?"

"Sure," I answered, because it would've been pretty darn hypocritical if I had said no after all that.

"Who was the woman that guy was asking for?"

"What guy?"

"The guy at the real estate office. He asked for some woman named Karen."

"Oh. I think she probably runs the place."

"The real estate office that's selling all our homes and stuff?"

"Right."

"How do you know that?" he asked.

Then I thought about all the things I could have said in response, like "I'm just guessing," or "Seems logical," or "I don't remember him even asking for anyone."

But if I was gonna have any chance of saving Daniel at all, I would first have to be honest.

And so I was.

"She's my mother."

chapter 13

ORANGE YOU GLAD I'M NOT MY MOTHER?

Now you're probably gonna want to ask me all sorts of questions about my mother, so let me just say this:

When my mother promised to take me to Punch's, she swore on my piñata's head.

And sure, maybe she wasn't breaking that promise when she put it off a week.

But when Punch's got torn down, *she broke that promise.*

And yeah, I know it's odd that my mom's the person putting all those spiky posts into the ground while I'm the one throwing them into the creek, but sometimes that's how the forces of the universe balance out.

And while I'm at it, let me just say that the worst saying ever is the one that goes, "The apple doesn't fall far from the tree." Which I think means a kid is a lot like the person who raised them. But that's really dumb because I would never break a promise like that. So in this case, the apple fell so far from the tree it rolled to the other side of the world and somehow became an orange.

Anyhow, after hearing how much Daniel's drawing room meant to him, it got me to thinking about some other way to stop the sale of his house.

And I mean, *really* thinking.

Like a knight planning for battle.

Who in their day would climb to the top of a castle turret to survey their lands and determine the strength of the approaching enemy, mostly by counting the number of banners they had.

And so I did the same, climbing the trellis behind our house to the roof, where I counted all the FOR SALE signs scattered around the neighborhood.

But I didn't do it alone.

For I brought along my life partner, Dr. Rutherford B. Hayes.

And before you get any ideas about taking a
turtle onto your roof—DON'T.

Because for one thing, you're not a knight. And
for another, my turtle is as nimble as a monkey.

Also, I wanted to be extra nice to him because
I had been spending all my time with Daniel. And
I know I told you that my life partner mostly liked
being alone, but he also liked being appreciated. And
when it came to a perceived slight, Dr. Rutherford B.
Hayes could be as delicate as blown glass.

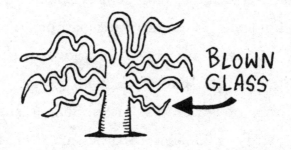

BLOWN
GLASS

Anyhow, the point is that I thought I'd make it up to him by giving him this high perch and asking for his advice.

Which worked.

Too well.

Because if there's one thing he loved, it was someone seeking his wisdom.

And sure enough, as soon as I lifted him onto the chimney, he poked his head out of his shell and began offering so many opinions it was hard to keep up.

Which might sound helpful.

But it wasn't.

Because not one of the topics he raised was germane to the situation.

And so I had to listen as he discussed:

Beets, gold, gills, film, stamps, stumps, lungs, kings, kin, kale, art, darts, racing, bathing, running, taking, giving, satin, silk, milk, bridges, wrinkles, sprinkles, ballets, ballrooms, ball gowns, opera, onyx, oryx, orcas, dances, lances, Shamu, shavers, shin guards, shampoos, Shawshank, Christmas, isthmus, wish lists, fish lips, pool dips, day trips, domes, dams, diving, driving, dining, truth, shoes, fur, law, saws, spoons, loons, moons, glue, pasta, post-cards, rainbows, Rome, Reims, Rio, rugby, raisins, ruins, rice, rain, rafts, rifts, roofs, cups, cliffs, clouds, wine, foes, ice, lice, anger, danger, rangers, dentists, dendrites, night-lights, bright lights, Lite-Brites, yoga, Yoda, yawning, winning, lava, liver, louvers, Levi's, cable, kibble, housing, hooves, grooves, moves, trees, dimes, limes, travel, banjos, cobblers, comfort, condos, caring, Cairo, carbon, watches, witches, Wasatch, Sasquatch, finals, fennel, funnels, tunnels, and, finally, the British Chunnel.

Anyhow, when he was done, I was so tired I didn't even *think* to ask him about how to save Daniel's home.

Because I don't know about you, but when I get tired, I forget just about everything.

And so I picked up Dr. Rutherford B. Hayes, who, having been given the opportunity to show off his smarts like that, felt like a million bucks.

And I walked down the roof with him, his dignity restored.

Which was when I remembered another trait of mine when I am tired:

Clumsiness.

Which was right about when I dropped him.

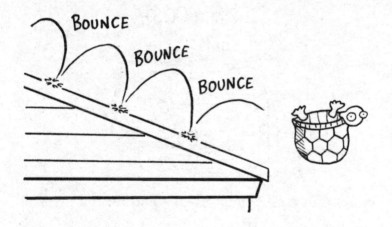

BOUNCE

BOUNCE

BOUNCE

chapter 14

SKELETON KEY

Dr. Rutherford B. Hayes landed perfectly in an ice-cold cooler of fresh lemonade.

And I mean *perfectly*.

SPLOOSH

As though in a past life, he had been a diver off the cliffs of Acapulco.

And I'm telling you, if I had *tried* to throw him

into that lemonade, I couldn't have done it if you had given me a thousand and one chances.

So physically he was fine.

Emotionally was a whole different matter. For he was not happy about the humiliation of bouncing down the roof like an orange.

Now the good news was that I was the only person who saw it.

That is, if you don't count Daniel, who was waiting for me on the front lawn holding that cooler of lemonade.

Though I don't think I told you why.

So let me back up.

You see, despite Daniel and his uncle having all their stuff packed up and being ready to move, their house still had not sold. And although I wanted to believe it had something to do with our storming of Chuck Les, the truth was that I didn't really know.

All I knew for sure was that his uncle was getting nervous, especially given the fact that he had already taken a writing job in another town. And so he told

Daniel that he had to keep the house especially clean for any potential buyers who might want to drop in and have a look.

And that meant he couldn't have any friends over.

Which meant me.

So if Daniel and I were going to continue to meet at his house, we had to make sure his uncle didn't find out. And thus we devised a system of communication for when his uncle was and was not home. And the system we worked out was this:

When his uncle was home, Daniel would tap three times on his bedroom window with the end of his cane.

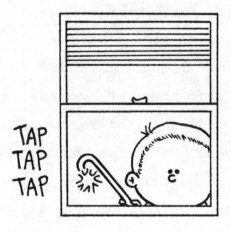

TAP
TAP
TAP

When his uncle was *not* home, Daniel would do this:

Only it didn't quite go as well as hoped. Because once when his uncle was home, Daniel grabbed his cane and tapped on the window so hard he did this:

And Daniel got into a lot of trouble for it, because his uncle was trying very hard to sell the home, and broken windows did not help make it more appealing to buyers, even if those buyers were probably gonna tear it down anyway.

And that's when I had a brilliant idea.

LIGHTBULB TO SYMBOLIZE BRILLIANT IDEA

And that idea was this:

If buyers were already hesitant about buying the home, we could do our part by making the situation worse.

Much worse.

So on a day when his uncle was gone, we set up what we called a "Consumer Information Station" right outside of that same broken window, where we offered free lemonade (the cooler that my turtle plopped into). And helpful advice.

"Aren't you worried your mom is going to see you out here?" asked Daniel.

"No," I answered. "She's at work."

"What if somebody tells her?"

"So what if they do? Nobody knows it's me. Why do you think I'm wearing my helmet again?"

"Smart," he said. "But what would she do if she *did* find out? I mean, not just about what we're doing here, but, you know, what we did at the office and all that."

"Daniel, life is filled with What-If Dragons. I'm here to slay them."

"Right," he said.

But I could tell he still wasn't persuaded. Especially because of what he said next.

"But what if, like, we *don't* succeed and I have to move to some strange place and I can never be in my house again?"

I waved my lance. "I hereby slay that What-If Dragon with my pointy lance. Because by the time we're through today, not a person on earth is going to want to buy this house."

And as soon as I said it, we were approached by two persons.

BAD HOUSE. DON'T BUY.

"Hey, pardon me, guys," said the man. "But are your parents home?"

Daniel shook his head. "It's my uncle's house."

"Oh, well, my girlfriend and I are wondering if we can get a quick look at the place."

"What for?" I asked.

"We're moving into the neighborhood. Just looking for something to buy."

"Big mistake," I told him.

Then he laughed. Which was insulting.

And he said this, which was even *more* insulting:

"Nice helmet there. Is it Halloween already?" Then he *and* his girlfriend laughed. Like that was some sort of high comedy.

Speaking of which, it's amazing how many stupid things adults laugh at. Maybe it's just because they're nervous and can't think of anything else to do, or maybe it's just what you're supposed to do when you're old and have hair growing out of your ears. But I'll tell you this—when I get older, you'll never see *me* laughing at jokes that aren't funny.

Anyhow, it really got us off on a bad foot. And so I said something I probably shouldn't have said.

YOU SHOULD
KNOW THIS
WAS ONCE
A NUCLEAR
TESTING
SITE.

And I don't know why I had to go so big with that particular lie. Especially when a simple one would have been fine.

Though maybe it was because the man could clearly see the broken window behind me and still wasn't discouraged. So I thought—well, *try harder*.

"Oh yeah?" he asked.

"Yes," I answered. "In fact, if you ever see my colleague and I at night, you'll see that we glow like fireflies."

"We'll have to be careful of that," he said.

But I could tell he didn't mean it. And I hated

being humored by any person who thought he was smarter than me. Because he wasn't. And I had a turtle that was probably seven hundred times smarter than both of those two people put together. So I said something else I probably shouldn't have said.

"Well, do what you want. Just know this house was built over an old graveyard."

And that seemed to get through to the woman, because the smile dropped from her face faster than crumbs from a slice of avocado toast.

"Are you being serious?" she asked.

"Babe, she's just having fun," said the man to the woman.

"I'm not," I said.

"Okay, no, seriously," said the woman. "That creeps me out."

And I could tell right there that the man felt Daniel's house slipping from his grasp, so he did something that even I have to admit was kinda smart.

He talked to Daniel.

"You live here?" he asked Daniel.

And before I could stop him, Daniel said, "Yes. And I don't want to move."

Which was the exact *wrong* thing to say. Because then the man said:

"But aren't you scared of the big, bad graveyard below you?"

And then he had Daniel trapped.

Because if Daniel said no, it would be like we were lying about the graveyard. And if he said yes, then it didn't make sense why he wanted to stay in the darn house.

And seeing my Daniel in Distress lose this battle of wits was more than I could take.

So I defended him.

"He *is* scared," I answered. "Very scared. That's why he wears steel-toe boots when he walks through the backyard."

"Steel-toe boots?" asked the woman, who was much easier to excite. "What for?"

"So he doesn't trip on any skeletal hands that might be poking out of the ground."

"Stop it!" yelled the woman. "Just stop it! You're making all this up."

"I wish," I answered.

"She *is* making all this up," said the man to his girlfriend. "And it's ridiculous. There are no hands coming up from the ground." Then he turned to us and said, "Now are your parents home or not?"

"Uncle," Daniel corrected him.

"Whatever," said the man.

"Let's just leave," said the woman, whirling around and folding her arms over her chest. "Creepy little kids."

But then her fear turned to anger, and she turned to me.

"Let me guess—this is your best friend's house. And the dilapidated one across the street is yours. And you don't want to see your best friend move."

Which was more or less true. Though I would quibble with some of the details.

"Is that what you're afraid of?" she continued. "People with money turning a neighborhood no one likes into one that people do? Well, if it's any consolation, I don't think anyone would ever buy *your* house."

And just when it looked like she was done, she remembered one more thing.

"Oh, and your little cardboard outfit? It looks ridiculous."

"Baby, c'mon," said the man as he put his arm around her and led her away from the table. "Let's just go talk to their parents."

"Uncle," said Daniel.

And seeing the woman's back turned, I did something that a knight of the round table could never do.

But that the Winged Skull o' Doom could.

I grabbed her ankle.

And as she ran off screaming, I couldn't help hurling one curse:

"May you never find a neighborhood as nice as ours."

chapter 15

UDDER HAPPINESS

The afternoon I spent at the Consumer Information Station taught me that each potential buyer had their own particular sensitivities.

Sensitivities that could be plucked like the strings of a jester's lute.

Like the person I told:

And the person I asked:

And the person to whom I said:

But after fighting all those noble battles, I was tired and hungry.

And we all know how I get when I'm hungry.

And so Daniel and I took down our Information
Station and went inside to the kitchen, where Daniel
grabbed two burritos that his uncle had left for him
in the fridge. One marked SHRIMP and one marked
VEGGIE.

"Which one do you want?" asked Daniel.

"Veggie," I answered. "I can never eat anything
with a face. Even beady-eyed little shrimp."

And so we sat on the floor of Daniel's chair-less
kitchen and ate our burritos.

And said nothing.

And you know you're really becoming close to
someone when the two of you can just sit there and
not say all this stupid stuff about things that don't

matter. Like how adults talk about the weather and their shoes.

And that brings me to something else which this may or may not be the place to discuss.

And that's this:

I think all any of us really wants is to just not be so alone. And if we're *really* lucky—to even be loved. Though that's not something you should go around expecting—because if you ask me, that's greedy.

Anyhow, that's all a long way of telling you that I was pretty darn happy just eating burritos with Daniel.

Maybe even better than happy.

Because I gotta say, seeing how Daniel chewed his food made him just about the most irresistible human being I had ever seen in my life.

And I'm not exaggerating.

I mean, it was sort of like a cow, if you want to know the truth. Like how they chew with their lower jaw swaying from side to side, and how some of the food falls out of their mouth. I first noticed it when he was eating those fries at The Beefy Bee, but it was *really* apparent with the burrito.

And maybe that doesn't sound attractive to you, but for me, it was love.

Mostly because it was so earnest.

Like it was the best thing Daniel had ever eaten.

And he didn't care how he looked doing it.

And when you find somebody like that in life, you gotta keep a close eye on them and not let them wander to wherever that big party is, the one filled with all the people you once knew—the one you're never invited to.

And so I kept a close eye on Daniel.

And that's when his uncle came home.

chapter 16

SHOWING CHARACTER

One thing you learn about adults after a while is that they never stay put.

Put them one place, they go another.

Put them here, they go there.

And so when Daniel's uncle said he was going away for the day, he apparently didn't mean it.

And that meant we had to flee.

Because if Daniel's uncle found me over at their house, who knew *what* would happen.

"Follow me!" Daniel said, suddenly grabbing me by the hand.

And soon we found ourselves in his bedroom, where he swung open his closet door.

"Get in!" he said.

"Your closet?" I answered. "He'll find us for sure!"

"Not where we're going," he said, climbing the shelves that lined the back of the closet toward a square hole in the ceiling. And using his cane to shove aside the wooden board over the opening, he turned back toward me. "Attic," he said. "He doesn't know I go up here."

And so I followed him into the attic, after which he made sure to slide the wooden board back into place, just as we heard his uncle enter his room.

"Daniel?" he said. "You home?"

So we stayed perfectly quiet until we heard his uncle's departing footsteps. And after we were sure he was gone, Daniel tiptoed to the slatted attic vent, through which he stared out into his front yard.

"He's here with some people," Daniel said.

"Who?" I whispered.

"I don't know," he answered. "They're hard to recognize from here."

And so I tiptoed to the vent and looked through the slats for myself.

And there I saw a woman my mother worked with at Chuck Les Homes, along with two people who at first I didn't recognize, and could hardly believe it when I did.

"It's the woman whose ankle I grabbed!" I told Daniel. "And the man she was with."

"No."

"Yes."

"How can that be?"

"Lattes," I answered. "They must give you great strength."

And so the two of us listened in silence as they entered the house, and the woman from Chuck Les said all sorts of dumb stuff about how big the lot was and how the neighborhood was really "up and coming," whatever that meant.

And if you want to know the truth, I got so caught up in what they were all saying that I almost missed the look of fear on Daniel's face.

Fear when the couple said they loved the neighborhood.

Fear when they asked when they could close the sale.

Fear when they said they might tear down the house.

And they were fears that my cardboard shield could not protect him from.

Which made me just about the most useless knight ever.

And so I wanted to rush over and put my arm around Daniel. Or cover his ears. Or even just go downstairs myself and tell that couple all about the nuclear test planned for that afternoon.

But it was no use.

Because I couldn't stop Daniel from hearing what he had already heard.

And so when the real estate agent led Daniel's uncle and the couple into the backyard and it felt safe for us to once again whisper, I tried to think of just the right thing to say.

And I don't know about you, but in my experience, that right thing never comes. Except after a week or so. And then you come up with this ridiculously brilliant thing to say that no longer matters because the world has moved on.

That's why if I ever find one of those magic lamps with the genie inside, my one wish is gonna be:

CAN I BE BRILLIANT IN THE MOMENT JUST ONCE?

Which probably isn't even something you're allowed to ask for. 'Cause when it comes to genies, I think you have to ask for a new pony or palace or truck.

But it turned out I didn't need to say anything at all.

Because out of the blue, Daniel said this:

And that's the thing about Daniel.

His mind is like this rabbit racing through a field. You just never know where it's gonna end up.

"Really," he said. "And sometimes you care about them even *more* than real people."

He stood up and walked to a spot where the sunlight from the vent was hitting the attic wall.

And there, for the first time, I noticed a drawing.

"This is Timmy," he said, pointing to the draw-ing on the wall. "We talk sometimes. I mean, he can't *really* talk—but sometimes it feels like he can."

"Did you draw that?" I asked.

"Yeah."

"It's good."

"It's okay. You're the first person I've shown it to."

Then he walked over to a small window on the other side of the attic and peeked from behind the drawn shade to make sure his uncle was still in the yard.

Which he was.

So Daniel continued.

"Maybe the reason I come up with characters is that they're the only people I know who can't leave me." He tapped the drawing of Timmy with his cane. "And now here I am leaving *them*."

And then, wouldn't you know it, someone in the street—probably one of the buyers—must have hit the alarm on their car by accident or something, 'cause suddenly all we could hear was this loud honking noise so obnoxious you wanted to pull your ears off.

And that's the thing about life—it has this way of screwing up the most beautiful moments. Almost like some superpower looks down and sees all that beauty and says, "Oh, no, better mess *this* moment up."

But then the alarm ended. And Daniel kept going.

"Anyhow, that's why I don't want to leave."

"So you've drawn other characters?" I asked.

He nodded. "I come up with a new one every time I'm sad. Or hurt. Or lonely."

And that's when he turned on the lightbulb over our heads.

And an entire wall was illuminated.

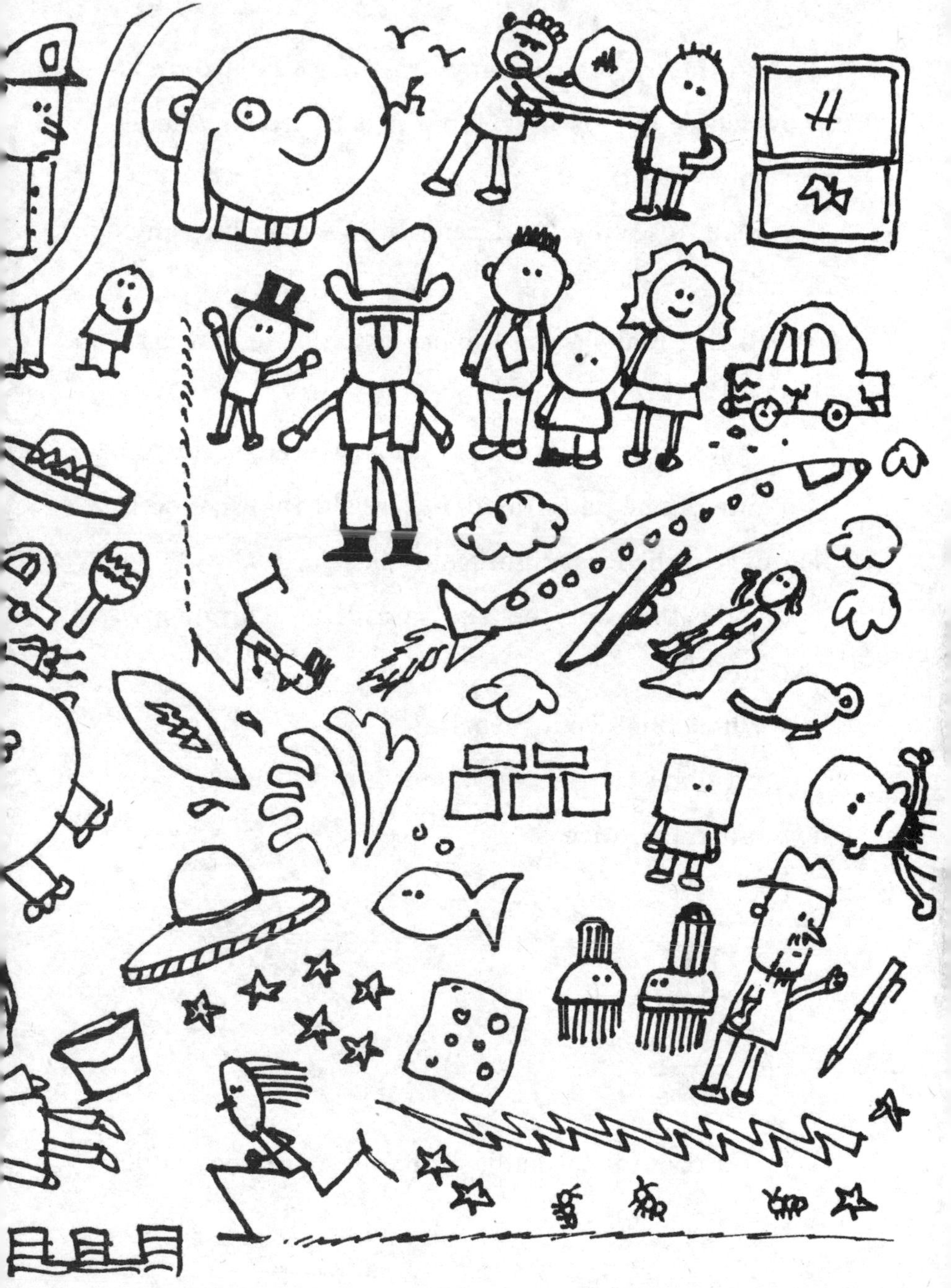

And there were so many drawings that I didn't know where to look first. "So *this* is the room where you draw," I said.

"Yeah. It's quiet. And peaceful. Do you like any of them?"

Which I really wasn't expecting him to just ask like that.

"I guess that pig over there," I answered, pointing to a cute pig he had drawn, but afraid that maybe I had picked the least significant one.

"I like that one too," he said. "But it's not my favorite."

"Which one's your favorite?" I asked.

And that's when he pointed to one I had somehow failed to notice:

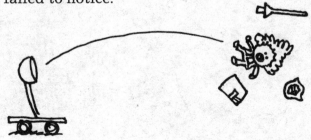

"You drew it!" I said, probably a bit too loud.

"Me flying out of a catapult! And you didn't make my hair smooshed or anything!"

I touched the drawing with my hand.

"You really did capture my essence."

Daniel smiled.

And, encouraged by our bonding over the pig, I then uttered something that was so dumb I wanted to just bang my head against the attic wall for the rest of the year. And I mean the whole year. Just stay up in the attic and make that my sole purpose in life.

Anyhow, the thing I said was this:

"I really liked it when you held my hand."

Then he just stared at me.

"Huh?" he asked.

And right then I knew I was sinking like a lead weight in Dr. Rutherford B. Hayes's aquarium. Because it meant Daniel didn't even know what I was talking about.

"When we ran out of the kitchen," I said, trying to rescue the little that was left of my waning dignity, "you held my hand."

"Oh," he said. "Right."

Right.

And suddenly desperate and drowning, I tried to rescue myself by changing the subject.

"I really like your cane."

Which didn't go well either.

Because all he said was:

"Why?"

Sorta like I had said I enjoyed getting struck by lightning.

"I dunno," I said. "I just think it's sorta beautiful."

"Oh," he said.

Oh.

Then he grabbed what was left of my burrito and started eating it.

Which I thought was a little odd.

But I was so relieved to be done talking about canes and hand-holding that I would have gladly fed him that burrito by hand.

Though I did say:

"Not that it matters, but I think that's my burrito."

But he shook his head.

"This one's mine," he said, showing me the shrimp inside.

"Then where's mine?" I asked. "I brought mine up here too."

Only it turned out that I hadn't.

Instead, I had dropped it onto the closet floor when I was watching Daniel escape into the attic.

Which, if you think about it, is a pretty odd spot for a burrito to be lying.

Which is exactly what his uncle thought.

chapter 17

DON'T COME 'ROUND HERE NO MORE

The worst part about Daniel's uncle finding us was not his discovery of me. It was the discovery of *our sign*, which we had stupidly left on Daniel's bed, just lying there for anyone to see.

BAD HOUSE.
DON'T BUY.

All of which was then made worse by the buyers, who apparently told Daniel's uncle everything we had said at the Consumer Information Station. Because if there's one thing you can count on from latte-sippers, it's a kick in the head when you're down.

And we were *down*.

Especially Daniel, who had no choice but to sit there while his uncle yelled.

Yelled about how ungrateful Daniel had been.

Yelled about how selfish he'd been.

Yelled about how deceitful he'd been.

Which was bad enough to take. But that wasn't even the toughest part.

That occurred when his uncle saw all the drawings in the attic and said there was no way they could sell the house with a kid's scribbles all over the walls, and so they were gonna have to hire someone to paint over them.

And that made my heart just about break into two.

And I know there's no excuse for this, given that I'm a knight and we're supposed to be courageous and bold, but when I heard that part, I fled out the front door and never stopped running.

Not because I was afraid. But because I didn't want Daniel to see me cry.

And I didn't run across the street to my home, because there was some small part of me that thought maybe his uncle didn't know where I lived. So instead, I just ran down the block.

Away from their house.

Away from my house.

Away from everything.

And the most embarrassing part was that I still had my shield. Which now seemed just about as useless as me.

And let me just say right here—have you ever noticed how, when you're the most scared and helpless, life seems to know it? And it picks just that moment to pounce and make it worse?

Well, it's true.

Which is why when I ran past The Beefy Bee, I saw this sign out in front:

And that made me so sad I just sat outside at one of the round tables and pouted.

And a knight is never supposed to pout at the round table.

And I don't mean I pouted a little. I pouted until it got so dark I could barely see my own feet.

After which I wandered home, hoping that that same darkness would allow me to slip into my house undetected.

Only when I got home, I realized that my mother was at some banquet for her real estate office. So I skipped the pork-and-beans dinner she had left for me on the kitchen counter and just went straight to my room.

Heat for 2 min in microwave.

Because I wasn't hungry.

For I knew that by now, Daniel's uncle had no doubt called her and spilled the beans, and probably the pork.

And that when she got home, I was going to be in a whole lot of trouble.

And Dr. Rutherford B. Hayes wasn't much help either. Because he was still sore about being dropped off the roof, which, frankly, I could understand. And that left me with no choice but to go into the closet and be with my rescue piñatas.

But even that didn't make me feel better. Because as soon as I started talking with them, guess who chimed in?

Dr. Rutherford B. Hayes!

Claiming we were talking too loud and were keeping him up.

Now I've talked to my rescue animals about a billion times, and my life partner has never once said we talked too loud. So that's how you know he was still upset about the whole roof thing.

So I marched right past that aquarium and didn't say a word to him. Because I wanted him to know *I* could be grumpy too.

And I went outside and climbed onto the roof and stomped on it extra loud—so he could hear it all the way down in my room—and did that until I got to the very top, where I sat on the ridge.

And heard:

"Gosh darn baby bell!!"

Now I don't know if there's a list of things you least expect to hear when you're sitting on your roof at night, but if there is, "Gosh darn baby bell" has to be on it.

And it came from somewhere behind me.

Now you're probably not gonna believe this next part, but I promise on the shell of Dr. Rutherford B. Hayes that it's true:

In all the times I had been on my roof, I had never

once looked at the house behind ours. I had always just stared out at Daniel's.

So for the first time ever, I turned around. And there in a lawn chair on the roof of her house was Old Lady Trifaldi.

Who, after her mansion was torn down, must have crossed town and moved into the small house behind ours. Upon the roof of which she was now eating cheese.

And it was only later that I learned she was not saying "baby bell," but "Babybel," a kind of cheese that comes in little round containers.

One of which she had dropped.

Whereupon it promptly rolled all the way to the ground.

"Why do the dumb little things have to be round? They should be *square. Square things don't roll!*"

Now I don't know what proper roof etiquette is, but I figured the polite thing to do was pretend I didn't hear her.

Which she made difficult.

"What—you don't have an opinion?"

"Who, me?" I asked.

"Do you see anyone else on these roofs?"

Which I didn't.

"I don't really know what you're talking about," I answered.

"Round cheese. For or against?" she summed up.

"I don't know. I just came up here to think."

Which I thought would be the end of the matter, but it wasn't.

"Think about what?" she asked.

And then I didn't know *what* to say. Though I tried to be polite.

"No offense, but—"

"AH!" she cut me off. "Don't say it!"

"Don't say what?"

"Whatever you're about to say next. Because whenever anyone says 'no offense,' the next thing they say is always offensive."

Which was funny, because that was something *I* always said.

And I don't know if it was our bonding over that phrase or just my desperation, but for some reason I blurted out exactly what I had been thinking about.

"I want to make time move backward."

And she said:

"Then let me show you how."

chapter 18

SEEING
THE LIGHT

It was a lot easier getting onto Mrs. Trifaldi's roof than onto mine.

And that was because she had a tall ladder set up in her driveway, the bottom of which was surrounded by fallen Babybels.

Of which she had dropped many.

And so I brought them to her in a bucket I found in her garage.

And I told her how sad I was about everything that had changed. Like with the neighborhood and her old house and Punch's and The Beefy Bee and Muffins and Sparrow and Daniel.

And I told her about Dr. Rutherford B. Hayes and my rescue piñatas and broken windows and the graveyard and nuclear tests and spiky posts and fake birthdays and praying knights and dead dragons and shields and lemonade and attics and canes and Chuck Les and Timmy and clowns and cafés and, I'm telling you, I told her *everything*.

And when I was done, she said:

"Gosh darn Babybel!"

Because she had dropped more cheese.

"They really need to start making them square," she added.

She grabbed another from the bucket.

"Do you know how many times I've seen this neighborhood change?" she asked.

I shook my head.

"A *lot*," she said. "At least every dozen years. And how old am I?"

"I don't know."

"I don't know either," she said. "I was hoping one of us did."

She bit into her cheese.

"Anyhow, every time things change, I think to myself how much I'd like them to go back to how they were."

"Me too," I replied.

"Cheese?" she asked, holding out a Babybel.

"No thanks," I answered.

"Go ahead," she said. "Cheese makes you wise."

So I took it.

And promptly dropped it down the roof.

"*See?*" she said. "Stupid things should be square! SQUARE, SQUARE, SQUARE!"

And, trying to make the best of a bad situation, I said:

"Maybe whoever makes them doesn't intend for them to be eaten on roofs."

"Whose side are you on?" she asked.

"They should be square," I replied.

"Right," she said. "Anyhow, every time things

change, I come up here and stare at those stars over our heads."

I looked up at the sky, which was filled with more stars than I had ever seen.

"The stars?" I replied. "I don't even like the stars. I'm always afraid they're gonna fall on our heads."

"You just need an umbrella."

Which was the same joke my mother had made. Only Mrs. Trifaldi seemed serious.

"Anyway," she continued, "you're missing the point. Stars aren't bad. They're good."

"What for?" I asked.

"To make time go backward. Isn't that what you asked for?"

"Yeah. But I don't get it."

"Well, there's a chance it only makes sense in my own brain. And that's the same brain that tells me to eat cheese on the roof."

"It's good cheese," I answered.

"Better if it was square," she said.

She took another bite.

"Anyhow," she continued. "See that big star right up there?"

"Which one?"

"The really bright one. Right over your head."

"Yeah," I said, finally spotting it.

"So that light—the light that's hitting your eyeball right this second—is from many years ago."

"It is?"

"Yeah, well, don't quote me—I'm not an astrologist or astronomist or whatever they're called. But yes, that light is from many years ago. Because that's how long it takes the light to reach us. Sometimes ten years. Sometimes a hundred years. Sometimes even a million years."

"Really?"

"Yup," she said.

She took another bite of her cheese.

"So every time you look up at a star, you're looking at the past," she continued. "Right there in front of you."

"I didn't know that," I said.

"Now you do," she answered. "Helps me to remember that even though things change, the past is still right there with us."

And I don't know why—maybe because we were

sharing and all—but I suddenly felt the need to tell her my *own* philosophy of life.

"I think all the people we once knew but are now gone all went to some big party and they're all there talking to each other."

"You believe that?"

"Yes," I answered. "Why?"

"Because that's what *I* believe," she said.

"Really?"

"Really."

"But then for some reason we're never invited," I continued. "Or our invitation got lost in the mail or something. So we can't go."

"Oh," she said. "That's where we differ."

"Why? What do you think?"

"I think we get to go."

"And see them?"

"Yup," she said. "Just like we see those stars."

She smiled.

"The past always present."

chapter 19

EXIT THROUGH
THE GIFT SWAP

When I got back home, my mother's car was not yet in the driveway.

So I crawled into bed even though I wasn't tired, thinking that if my mother suddenly came home, I could fake like I was sleeping and at least put off my punishment for another day.

But maybe I was more tired than I'd thought, because when I opened my eyes, it was already morning.

And I had missed my mother again. And if her note was any indication, she had not yet heard what had happened.

> Missed you,
> Sleepyhead.
> Breakfast
> on table.
> xo

And suddenly I felt like I was the queen of the world.

Why? Because if my mother didn't know what had happened by that point, it meant Daniel's uncle was probably not going to tell her. And maybe that was because he wanted us to be on good terms. And the only reason he'd want *that* is if we were going to be neighbors for a long time. And that meant he had not yet sold the house.

So maybe that couple had had second thoughts after all.

All of which meant that Daniel wasn't going any-where soon. And news like that can make a knight walk with a certain spring in her step.

And so I gave an extra morning pat to each of my rescue animals.

And said something to Dr. Rutherford B. Hayes that I should have said long ago:

And, after eating my breakfast, I even did the dishes.

Because even though my mother hadn't found out what I'd done, I felt I owed *her* an apology too.

And when you're doing that many kind things in a row, the universe often pays you back with some sort of gift. Sort of its way of saying, "Way to go, kiddo."

And when I walked outside, that gift was on my porch.

Along with a note.

A
beautiful
Cane for
You!
—Daniel

And maybe this is the dumbest thing you've ever heard, but I actually *hugged* that cane.

Because I don't know about you, but I never get gifts for no reason. They're pretty much limited to birthdays and special events.

So for Daniel to think of me like that was probably the most extraordinary thing that had ever happened in my life. And it was so exciting that I'd missed the best part of the note. The P.S. on the back.

And I don't know if there was anyone around to see what happened next, but I actually started *floating* down my walkway.

Which maybe you think isn't possible. But it turns out that it is.

And it made me want to write my own note back to Daniel.

And I knew exactly what I wanted to say.

Which reminds me.

I don't think I ever told you what Muffins did the last time I ever saw him.

And if I did, stop me.

Anyhow, I had gone to the store to just buy a book, which he slipped into a bag.

And when he left, he said the same thing he always said, which was, "Don't slam the darn door, dingo."

But when I got home, I opened the bag with my book in it, and down at the bottom was the most beautiful knight I'd ever seen.

Courtesy of Muffins.

Along with a note:

HOMEWORK FINITO?

And that's about the only other time I can ever remember somebody giving me a gift for no reason—although I guess you could say it was sort of Muffins's goodbye gift. Because he probably knew the store was gonna get torn down and just didn't want to tell me.

Anyhow, that's how Daniel's gift made me feel, only a hundred times better.

Which is why I was floating like a butterfly all the way across the street.

Right toward Daniel's house.

Where I saw something new atop their FOR SALE sign.

Something that made me see the cane for what it actually was.

A goodbye gift.

chapter 20

RAISING CANE

I can't tell you everything that happened next, because to tell you the truth, it's all a bit hazy. Sorta like that fog-of-war thing I read about in one of my knight books.

Which was ironic.

Because I was hurling every one of those knights against the wall of my room.

Which must have come as quite a surprise to them, kneeling as they were in hopeful prayer.

And the dragons fared even worse.

For after I threw them, I stomped on them for good measure.

And for once I was pretty sure they did not die of old age.

And the dragons didn't even get the worst of it.

That was saved for my helmet and shield, which I tore into just about a thousand pieces.

And believe me, that sort of display is gonna get noticed by your life partner.

Who rose from the water in his tank and did everything he could to calm me down.

But I don't think I even *heard* what he was saying. Because when you're lost in the fog of war, you miss a lot of things.

And if you think all this sounds really bad, let me tell you right now that I haven't even gotten to the very worst part.

And I know I've made a whole lotta mistakes and told you about most of them, but really, this was the very worst one.

So if you want to stop reading right now, it's fine with me.

Anyhow, it involved Daniel's cane.

No, I didn't break it.

Instead, I used it to break almost all the windows in his house.

Like the living room window.

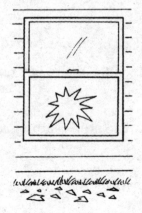

The kitchen window.

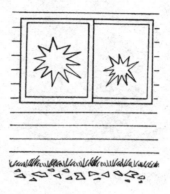

And every other window I could reach with that cane.

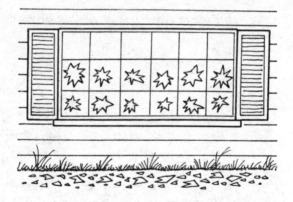

And after I was done, I threw the cane onto their front lawn and grabbed the SOLD sign.

And ran as fast as I had ever run down the middle of my street.

Past the remnants of Punch's.

Past the empty Beefy Bee.

Past the condescending gazes of the latte-sippers.

Until I got to the creek.

Where, in the light of day, indifferent to all caution and sense, I lifted the sign high overhead.

And saw my mother.

SOLD

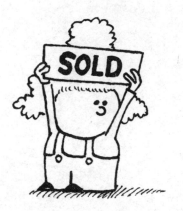

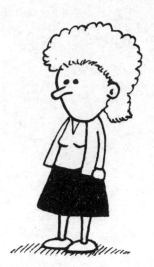

chapter 21

WINDOW TO THE SOUL

The first thing I have to tell you is that my mother didn't just see the one sign I was holding.

She saw *all* the signs.

And the second thing I have to tell you is that she was not pleased.

She was angry.

So angry she didn't yell.

But was silent.

And silence can sometimes be the worst form of yelling.

In fact, it wasn't until we were home and sitting in the kitchen that she even said a word.

And when she did, she spoke softly. And that somehow made it worse.

First she told me how hard it had been for her office to replace all those signs I had thrown into the creek. And how much money it had cost. And how frustrating it had been that it kept happening over and over. And to think, she went on, that the person who was causing all of it was living in her own house. *And was her own daughter.*

Not some vandal in the neighborhood.

Her own daughter.

A daughter that she had cared for and loved.

And this was how I thanked her.

This was how I showed appreciation.

And then the duck quacked.

QUACK QUACK QUACK

Not a real duck.

But a phone duck.

She had made it the ringtone of her phone once to make me giggle, but then she couldn't figure out how to change it back.

"I have to take this," she said, turning to the phone. "Do *not* go anywhere."

Then there was a long silence while she listened to whoever it was. "No, I don't want to buy anything. . . .

No. I don't. . . . No. I am not interested. . . . No. I'm hanging up now. I'm hanging up. Goodbye."

"Stupid telemarketers," she said. "I'm waiting for a call, so I had to take it."

Then she turned back to me.

"Do you have any idea what my employer would do if they found out my daughter was the person stealing the signs?"

"I didn't *steal* them," I objected. "I just put them in the creek."

Which was just about the dumbest thing I could have said.

Because then she *did* start yelling.

"Do you think this is a game?"

And even though I knew it was wrong, I raised my voice too.

"You made Punch's disappear!"

"I what?"

"The toy store. They tore it down. They're gonna replace it with some stupid coffee shop."

"And how is that *my* fault?"

"It was your company that sold it."

"What?"

"Chuck Les. They're the ones who sold it."

"Saint, there are a ton of agents in my office. I don't know all their listings."

"It was my favorite toy store!"

"So this is about a *toy store*?"

"It wasn't just a toy store!"

"Saint, I'm very sorry they tore it down. But if you think you're going to get out of this by saying you were upset about a toy store, you are *mistaken*."

"It wasn't just the toy store. *Everything* is gone! Everything is changing! All the stuff I love! It's disappearing!"

"Saint, that happens everywhere! Places go away! New places come! In every town. Everywhere!"

"Wrong."

"What do you mean, wrong?"

"They happen because *you* make them happen!"

"Saint, I'm a real estate agent! That's my job," she said, pointing to all the files that she kept in the kitchen, which she sometimes used as an office. "I help people who want to sell homes and businesses. And *I* don't sell the properties. They do. And by the way, it's the income from that job that allows me to take care of *you*. For which you seem to have absolutely *zero appreciation*."

"But you're ruining everything."

"I'm not ruining anything! I don't even know what you're talking about! Do you have any idea how much money we owe? Hospital bills from the car accident that I'll be paying back for the rest of my life. So I have a job, Saint! A job that barely keeps us above water as it is! Can you understand any of that?"

"But I want Punch's to be right where it was."

"Is that what this is about?"

"Yes! I want Punch's back!"

"Is that what this is about?" she asked again.

"Yes! Right on the corner where it was!"

"Is that what this is about?" she repeated, moving closer to me.

"I want things to be like they were!"

"*Is that what this is about?*" she said, grabbing me by the shoulders, her trembling face almost touching mine.

And then I just started to sob.

And between sobs said something I had never said to her before.

"*I miss Dad.*"

And when I said it, my mother grabbed me with both her arms and held me just about as tightly as I'd ever been held by anyone.

"*I really miss him,*" I said again.

And I just kept crying.

"*I want everything to be like it was.*"

And for a long time, neither one of us said a word.

Until finally my mom took my face in her hands and said:

"Saint, if there was anything I could do to change that and bring him back to this world, I would. *But I can't.* Oh, sweetie. I promise you, I would do *anything.*"

But I just kept crying. *"I miss all those Sundays he took me to Punch's."*

"Oh, sweetie," she said, still holding me, rocking me. "Ohh, sweetie."

And then, wouldn't you know it, the duck quacked again.

"Arrrgh!" she grunted, grabbing the phone and trying desperately to make it stop. Which she couldn't. So she flung it across the room, where it landed in the couch cushions, which at least partially muffled the duck.

Then she knelt once again in front of me.

"Saint, instead of doing all the stuff that you did, which was bad—*really* bad—you should have just talked to me."

"I wanted to, but I couldn't."

"What do you mean, you couldn't?"

"You're never home," I said.

"Baby, you know I work."

"But I'm by myself all the time."

"Not *all* the time," she said. "I'm home at night."

"Well, a lot of the time."

"I'm sorry, sweetheart, but it's just me. I don't have anyone to help me. And I can't afford a nanny, or even a babysitter. And I'm responsible for you, for working, for everything."

"I hate being alone."

"Sweetie, I'm doing the best that I can."

"It makes me sad."

And I don't know if it was my admitting that or what, but then she paused, took a breath, and said:

"I'm sorry."

And stroked the top of my head.

"I'm so sorry."

And hugged me tighter.

"I will do better."

She stroked my head again. "I promise. I don't want you to be sad, sweetie. Not if I can help it. I'll do better. I promise you."

And for a second it looked like *she* was gonna start bawling too. And I didn't want us *both* to be bawling. So I tried to make her feel better.

"It's okay," I told her. "I'm not always sad. I have

Daniel." And then I added, "At least for now."

"Who's Daniel?" she asked.

"My friend."

"Have I met him?"

"I don't think so. I don't think I've introduced him to anybody."

"Who is he?"

"The boy across the street."

"Our street?"

"Yes," I said, pointing toward the kitchen window. "In the house right across from us."

And then she just stared at me. And stood.

And walked to the kitchen window, where she pulled open the blinds.

And turned back to me and said:

"Saint, there hasn't been a house there in ten years."

chapter 22

THERE'S ALWAYS A CHANCE

Like soil enriched by a flood, sometimes good flows from bad.

And as bad as getting caught by my mom was, the good that followed was better.

Like how she stopped going into the office every other Tuesday.

Not to do errands or work from home.

But to spend them with me.

A promise she made with her hand on the piñata.

And this time she meant it.

And she made sure to spend time with Dr. Rutherford B. Hayes as well.

Who, given his dislike of strangers, did not appreciate the immediate intimacy.

Though I knew that in time Dr. Rutherford B. Hayes would love it. Particularly as he now had double the audience for his wide-ranging sermons.

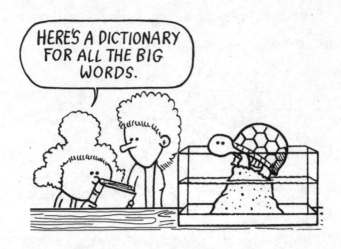

Which is not to say I wasn't punished for what I had done. And that meant cleaning my mom's office once a week for six months.

For which I was given just enough money to buy a repair kit for my knights, their prayers for aid finally answered.

Which was bad news for the dragons, who once again died of natural causes and poor hygiene like never before.

As for Daniel, I think it all comes back to what he said in the attic.

EVER NOTICE HOW IN A BOOK OR A MOVIE, A CHARACTER CAN BE AS REAL TO YOU AS SOMEONE YOU KNOW IN REAL LIFE?

Well, that's what Daniel was to me.

As real to me as you are to yourself.

Or I am to you.

And yes, the weed-filled lot across from us had been empty for a very long time. And was now for sale.

It was on the first block torn down by the people buying up our town. Though no one had built on it since.

Except me.

Which reminds me of something else Daniel told me that day in the attic.

And that was how he'd gotten his nickname.

Chance.

And it involved one of the only clear memories he had of his father.

Who had told him one day, "As long as you have your imagination in this life, you've got a chance."

Which really wasn't what Daniel's father told Daniel.

But what my father told me.

And thus I could have conversations with my turtle.

And my rescue piñatas.

And Daniel.

Who I now call Chance.

All of whom were with me every day.

For every moment alone.

And every moment I walked through a changing life.

And a changing city.

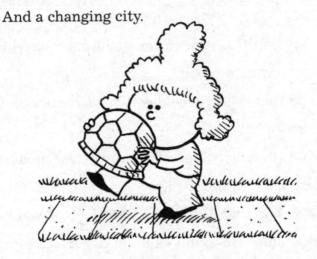

And as I walked, I thought of Mrs. Trifaldi and all the change she had seen in *her* long life, however long that had been. And how she took comfort from the stars. And her cheese.

Which made me hungry.

And so I went looking for somewhere new to eat.

And wouldn't you know it—maybe all that positive thought got noticed by the universe or something—because then I saw this:

How that happened, I had no idea.

And didn't much care.

All I knew was that The Beefy Bee was back.

And while there was no more Sparrow to be found at the order window, there was someone even better.

And I'm telling you, when I saw Muffins in that window, I wanted to hug his grumpy head right there.

Though he probably would have shut the window on my fingers.

So instead, I just ordered fries.

And I have to say they were quite good. For Muffins was almost as good at frying potatoes as he was at finding knights. And I was sure that one day, as he got better, he would serve me not only the fries I wanted—but the fries I *needed*.

Though his habit of spitting seeds while cook-
ing would not be sanctioned by any reputable health
department.

And the best part was that Muffins didn't seem
to care about how long I sat at the new square tables
outside.

Or that I put Dr. Rutherford B. Hayes on top of
one of them so he could read the Sunday Literary
Supplement.

And by the time my life partner was done reading, it was already night.

And so we walked home.

The knight with her trusty steed.

And while I may not have been victorious in

my battle against the latte-sippers, I had fought with enough honor to dub myself "Guardian of the Sacred Piñata."

A title I wore with pride as I made my way home.

A moment so perfect I knew there'd have to be a car alarm.

Only there wasn't.

There was just a faint cry in the distance.

And that's the thing about life—sometimes it lets a beautiful moment just be.

As we looked up at the stars.

The past always present.

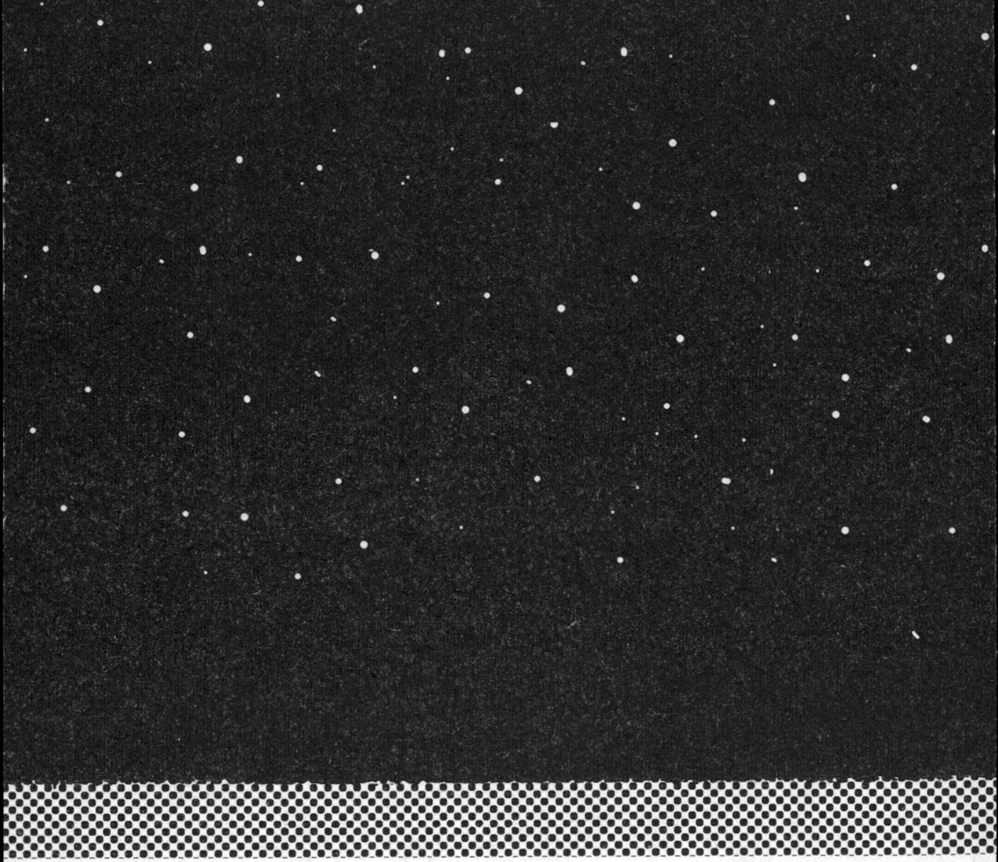

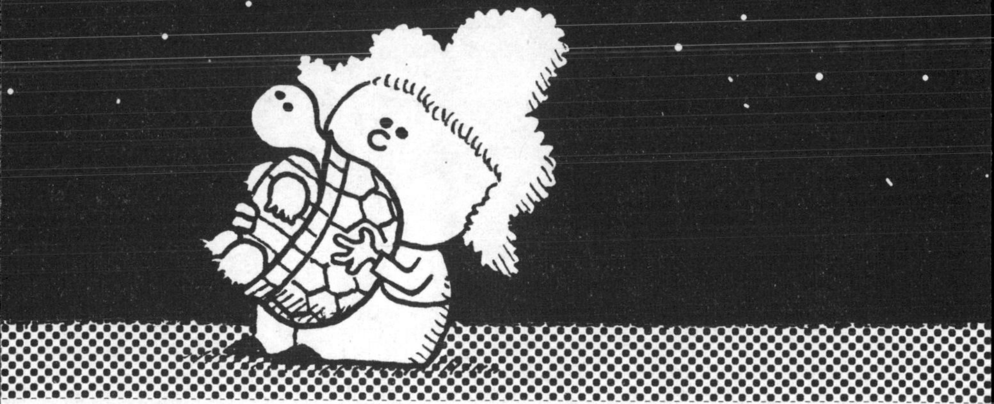

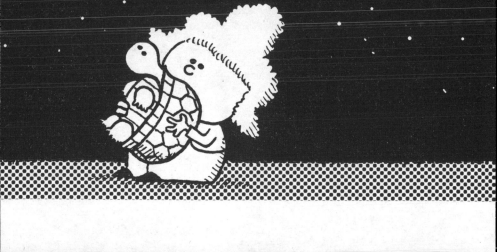

THE END

· Acknowledgments ·

Special thanks to Karin Paprocki for all her wonderful help with the art in this book. And to Kara Sargent for being the best editor ever.

STEPHAN PASTIS

is the creator of the syndicated comic strip *Pearls Before Swine*, which appears in over 800 newspapers. He is also the creator of the Timmy Failure book series and the cowriter of the Disney+ movie *Timmy Failure: Mistakes Were Made*. He lives in Northern California with his wife and two kids.